HORSE IN THE HOUSE

Mandy tightened her fingers on the barrier. Just three more of Wilfred's horses to be sold.

"That Newcombe man's bought Honey as well," James said. "He must have tons of money."

"I hope he's got enough left to buy William and Matty, too," Mandy responded, crossing her fingers for luck. *I'll give Matty a final hug when I give her the apple*, she thought.

The loudspeaker crackled into life again. "And now the last of the horses from Bennetts' Stables. William is a nine-year-old gelding. . . ."

Mandy's eyes widened in surprise. That couldn't be right. William wasn't the *last* of Wilfred's horses. There was still Matty to come.

"Hey! What's going on?" said James.

"I don't know," Mandy replied.

They waited expectantly while William was led around the sale ring. The auctioneer acknowledged the last few bids. "Any more? All done?" There came the sound of the auctioneer's hammer hitting wood again. "Sold to Mr. Newcombe. And that was the final horse from Bennetts' Stables . . ."

Mandy looked at James. "But what about *Matty*?"

Read all the Animal Ark books!

by Ben M. Baglio

$3.99 US Each!

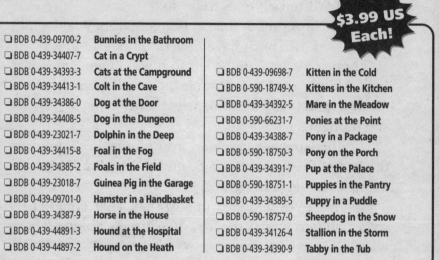

ANIMAL ARK®

Horse in the House

Ben M. Baglio

Illustrations by Jenny Gregory

AN
APPLE
PAPERBACK

SCHOLASTIC INC.

New York   Toronto   London   Auckland   Sydney
Mexico City   New Delhi   Hong Kong   Buenos Aires

ISBN 0-439-34387-9

25 24 23 22 21 20 19 18 17   5 6 7 8 9/0

Printed in the U.S.A.   40

Special thanks to Susan Bentley.
Thanks also to C. J. Hall,
B.Vet. Med., M. R. C. V. S., for reviewing
the veterinary information contained in this book.

One

"Here you are, Dad," Mandy Hope said, placing the bag of carrot sticks on the dashboard of the Land Rover. "I cut these up for you."

"How kind!" Adam Hope said with a grin. He eyed the carrots without much enthusiasm. "Oh, well. I guess they'll stave off the hunger pangs."

"Yes. And then you won't be tempted to stop and buy chocolate in Walton before we get to the horse auction!" Mandy said promptly.

Her dad was on a diet, but he was terrible at sticking to it. Above his dark beard, his face was red and shiny.

1

Earlier that morning, Mandy had heard him huffing and puffing on his exercise bike.

"Hear that, James?" Dr. Adam said. "She's got it all figured out."

James chuckled. "She usually does!"

Mandy's best friend sat in the backseat. He had been invited to go to the horse auction with Mandy and her dad, who was overseeing the horses for sale.

"All set?" Dr. Adam steered the Land Rover down the driveway and past the wooden sign that read, ANIMAL ARK, VETERINARY CLINIC.

"Have a good time!" Mandy's mom, Emily Hope, waved them off. She was standing outside the old stone house.

"Bye, Mom! See you later!" Mandy called out.

Emily Hope smiled, her long red hair stirring in the warm breeze.

"Oh! And good luck!" Mandy yelled with a grin.

With a final wave, Dr. Emily went into Animal Ark, where morning office hours were about to start. Mandy's parents were both vets with a joint practice in the town of Welford.

"Why did you wish your mom good luck?" James asked, looking puzzled.

"Because Mrs. Ponsonby's bringing Pandora in first thing this morning!" Mandy exclaimed.

"Yikes!" said James. "She's going to need it, then."

Mrs. Ponsonby was a large, imposing woman, who doted on her overweight Pekingese. Mandy imagined her sailing into the clinic, wearing one of her flowery hats, the little dog under one arm.

"You must look at my darling Pandora at once," Mandy said, in imitation of Mrs. Ponsonby's rich, bossy voice. "My precious one is looking extremely off-color."

"That Ponsonby woman," Dr. Adam said, shaking his head. "It's bound to be the usual story. Nothing wrong with Pandora that sticking to a sensible diet wouldn't cure."

"Hmm. Some people have no willpower," Mandy said. "Want a carrot stick, Dad?"

Dr. Adam coughed and gave his daughter one of his lopsided smiles.

The Land Rover went around a curve, and the house, with its modern vets' extension in the rear, disappeared from view. On the road that led up to the Fox and Goose crossroads, beautiful blossoms dotted the hedges.

"Don't you just love spring?" James said, looking out at the fields and at the lambs frolicking, their black tails flicking back and forth.

"Yup. Almost as much as having school vacation!" Mandy joked. "Isn't it great? We've got days and days to do anything we want to."

"Like spend them with the animals at Animal Ark," James said. "That's what you like to do best!"

Mandy smiled to herself. She knew it was what James liked best, too, even if he *did* sometimes pretend he was more interested in computers.

Dr. Adam drove into Welford, then slowed the Land Rover as the road out of the town climbed and narrowed into winding curves.

"There doesn't seem to be anyone at Bennetts' Riding Stables," Mandy said as they approached a little house that stood at the roadside on the outskirts of Welford.

Over the past month, she and James had been helping Wilfred Bennett out at the stables, while his wife, Rose, had been ill in the hospital. Sadly, Rose Bennett had died a few weeks ago. Mandy craned her neck. The fenced-in area beyond the house and the cluster of stable buildings looked forlorn and deserted. There was a FOR SALE sign up near the road.

"Look at that," said James. "They've put a 'Sold' notice over the sign!"

"Yes. Sam Western bought the Bennetts' land," Dr. Adam informed him. "He didn't waste any time. Knowing that man, he's already got plans for the place."

"But what will Wilfred do now?" Mandy was worried about their elderly friend. Surely Sam Western, the wealthy owner of Upper Welford Hall, wouldn't throw Wilfred Bennett out of his home.

"Don't worry," Dr. Adam said, munching away at a carrot stick. "Wilfred still has his house. He'll have a comfortable retirement. I expect we'll see him at the auction with his horses. They're up for sale today."

"Oh." A shadow was cast over Mandy's good mood. "Do all the Bennetts' horses have to be sold? Even dear old Matty? She was Rose's favorite."

Mandy was very fond of Matty, too. After she and James had learned to ride at Bennetts' Stables, Mandy had usually chosen the gentle silver-gray horse.

"I bet Wilfred hates having to sell Matty," James chimed in. "She was born at the stables, wasn't she?"

"Yes," Mandy agreed. "Rose said she delivered Matty herself."

As she imagined Rose Bennett bending over Matty, a newborn foal with long spindly legs and huge dark eyes, Mandy felt a tug at her heart. It was awful to think that they might never see Matty again after today's horse sale.

Dr. Adam glanced across at Mandy. "Don't look so glum, honey. I'm sure all the Bennetts' horses will find good homes, including Matty. And I'll be there to see that everything goes all right."

Mandy had a sudden idea. "Maybe Wilfred could keep

his horses — if he had an extra helping hand or two," she suggested. "James and I could keep helping with the chores around the stables," she said eagerly. "We wouldn't mind, would we, James?"

James nodded in agreement.

"I'm afraid that wouldn't make any difference," Dr. Adam said gently.

"What do you mean?" Mandy asked.

"Well," Dr. Adam explained, "it's not just help that Wilfred needs — it's money. The Bennetts gave away a lot of free riding lessons to people who couldn't afford them, such as groups of disabled children and adults."

"I remember," Mandy said. "That was really nice of them."

Dr. Adam nodded. "Yes, it was. Everyone in the area admired the Bennetts. But I'm afraid they've been too kind for their own good. They had no head for business and got into a lot of debt. The stables hadn't been paying their way for some time, but no one knew about it. It's only come out since Rose died. I was as surprised as anyone to hear about how much money Wilfred owes."

"Oh." Mandy felt sorry for Wilfred. First his wife had died, and now this. "He must have been so worried."

"But couldn't Wilfred have borrowed some money?" James asked, practical as usual. "People get bank loans for all kinds of things."

Dr. Adam shook his head. "Things had gone too far for that. The land had to be sold to pay off Wilfred's debts."

"So he doesn't have anywhere to keep horses now," Mandy stated, her spirits sinking into her boots. "Even if he wanted to."

Matty was very old now, she thought worriedly. The poor old thing might have difficulty settling into a new home. For one wild moment, Mandy thought of asking her dad if he would buy Matty, but she immediately dismissed the idea. Her parents had strict and sensible rules about having pets and taking in strays.

"Cheer up, Mandy. You have to get used to animals moving on." Dr. Adam's voice was kind, but firm. "As vets, we can't afford to get too attached to them."

"I know." Mandy nodded miserably. Her dad was right, but it wasn't always easy to take good advice.

The sunlit houses and farm buildings along the road to Walton sped by. Wildflowers were blooming at the roadside and the hills were ablaze with bright yellow flowers. Deep in thought, Mandy hardly noticed. The next thing she knew, they had driven into Walton and Dr. Adam was parking the Land Rover at the auction in the space reserved for the visiting vet.

"Wow! There are a lot of people here," James said.

"Yes," Mandy agreed, looking around at the horse

trailers and expensive-looking modern trucks that were packed closely together. Stable boys were ushering horses from their trailers and walking them back and forth to warm up their cramped muscles.

"Are you okay now, Mandy?" Dr. Adam said, ruffling his daughter's shortish hair.

She smiled up at him. "I will be, once I know that all the Bennetts' horses have gone to good homes."

"That's my girl. Look, there's Wilfred," Dr. Adam said, raising his hand to greet Wilfred Bennett as they approached the parking lot for the trucks.

Mandy saw that the old man's face looked sad and drawn. His straggly white hair was hidden beneath a checkered cap. He wore a tattered overcoat and wool muffler and his shoulders were hunched as if he was cold, although there was hardly even a breeze.

Despite the difficult situation, Dr. Adam and Wilfred shook hands warmly and exchanged a few words.

"Now then, you two young 'uns." Wilfred even managed a shaky smile for Mandy and James.

"Hi, Wilfred," they chorused.

"I didn't get much of a chance to thank you for helping me out at the stables over these past weeks while Rose was in the hospital," Wilfred said. He spoke slowly, as if the words were an effort, but he was determined to get them out. "I want you both to know that I really appreciated your help. I know Rose did, too. She was glad to know that the horses were in such good hands — especially her Matty."

"That's all right," said James. "We liked helping. Didn't we, Mandy?"

"Of course we did," Mandy replied. It had been hard work, but worth it, to see that the horses and ponies were comfortable.

Wilfred smiled, though his eyes were sad. "You two had some happy times at Bennetts', didn't you? Especially with our Matty. Though you weren't too keen to ride her at first, eh, James? Even though the dear old girl's as gentle as a lamb."

James flushed, then he grinned. "Mandy persuaded me to take riding lessons. I'm still not very good, but I enjoyed it."

Mandy had a lump in her throat and had to take a deep breath before she could speak. She swallowed hard and forced herself to look up at Wilfred. "I'm so sorry about Rose and I'm sorry that you have to sell your horses," she said, searching for the right words.

"Thank you. I appreciate your concern. I'm sorry, too," Wilfred said, the tight line of his mouth softening. "But there's no way around it. The horses have to be sold and that's the end of it."

Dr. Adam patted the old man's shoulder sympathetically, then said in his usual straightforward way, "Are you sure you're up to this, Wilfred? I can take care of things for you if you'd like me to. It's really no trouble."

Mandy realized that her dad meant to be kind, but somehow she knew that Wilfred was going to refuse his offer of help.

Wilfred lifted his cap and smoothed back his hair, then he set the cap more firmly on his head. "Thanks. I appreciate the offer, but I'm staying with the horses to see them on their way. I owe them that much."

"Fair enough. I understand," Dr. Adam said. "Well, then, I'd better get going. The auction's about to start. I'm needed for a while, but I'll make sure I see you before I leave."

"All right," Wilfred said shortly. The closed-up expression was back on his face. He nodded briefly at Mandy and James, then walked away.

Mandy stared after Wilfred until his stooped figure had been swallowed up by the crowd. She understood why he wanted to stay and see his horses sold, even if it did almost break his heart. She would have wanted to do the same thing.

"He's a proud old man," said Adam Hope. "They don't make them like that anymore."

Mandy and James followed Dr. Adam as he led the way toward the pens and the group of buyers who were gathering. He reached into the pocket of his coat, pulled out a typed list, and passed a cursory glance down the various names.

"Hmm. It's going to get pretty hectic around here once the bidding starts," he said to Mandy and James. "You two stay put behind the barrier. It's safest there and I'll know where to find you. I'll see you after the sale."

"Okay, Dad," Mandy said.

She and James found themselves a good viewing point near the sale ring. The holding pens, where the horses were examined and given some last-minute grooming by their owners, were some distance away. Mandy couldn't see where Wilfred Bennett was. He was probably over by the holding pens, too, she decided, spending every last moment he could with his horses.

"First today, we have Caesar, a three-year-old bay gelding." The auctioneer, a portly, red-faced man in a yellow vest, was up on the stand. He looked out over the buyers. "Who'll start the bidding?"

"Sold! To you, sir!" the auctioneer announced a few minutes later. His hammer hit the gavel and a buyer held up a card with his name written on it.

Mandy and James watched the stable boys lead the next few horses into the sale ring. Metal shoes rang on the hard ground as hooves clip-clopped around the circle within the barrier. As each horse was sold, another was brought into the ring.

Each time the auctioneer glanced at his list, Mandy expected to hear Matty's name over the loudspeaker.

"It's exciting, isn't it?" said James. "I mean, even though we feel sorry about Wilfred and everything."

Mandy nodded in agreement. "There are more horses here than at the Welford Show."

All kinds of horses could be seen, from mild-natured, sturdy Welsh ponies to sleek, hot-blooded Thorough-breds. *But none of them is as lovely as gentle, silver-coated Matty*, thought Mandy.

Two hours passed before Mandy glanced up at a wall clock. She was beginning to get hungry. She resisted the temptation to eat the apple that she had snatched quickly on the way out of Animal Ark and stuffed in her pocket. It was a good-bye treat for Matty.

"And now the first of a number of horses from the highly reputable Bennetts' Riding Stables."

"Here they come at last," said James. He didn't look excited now, just subdued and a little sad.

Mandy felt the same. She set her shoulders and looked over the barrier.

"We'll begin with Star — a ten-year-old mare."

As Star was led into the ring, Mandy saw the ripple of interest run through the buyers. "Who'll start the bidding?" the auctioneer asked again. Mandy tensed. This was it. It might be the last time she saw any of the Bennetts' horses, including Matty. She found herself longing to see her. The bidding for Star was fierce, with voices seeming to come from everywhere. Suddenly the hammer hit the gavel. "To you, sir!" And Star was sold.

"And now we have Socks. Also from the Bennetts' stable. Who'll start me at . . ."

Socks — with the two white feet — pranced around the ring, looking unconcerned about all the commotion. He, too, was sold quickly. Then came graceful Bella. The bids came fast, while the auctioneer noted each one, tapping at the air with his pen.

"Any more bids? Do we have the last bid? Sold to you, sir!"

"Goodness!" said James. "They don't waste any time, do they?"

"No," Mandy replied. "That's because Wilfred's horses are so good."

It was true. Muscles moved fluidly beneath the glossy coats, heads were held high, and ears pricked intelligently. Despite her feelings about the sale, Mandy felt proud for Wilfred. His horses were so beautiful. "A credit to him," her grandma would have said.

Mandy wished each horse luck. "Good-bye. I hope you'll be happy in your new home," she whispered.

Next to be announced was Wilfred's sturdy brown pony, Treacle. Treacle trotted around the ring, his tail swishing back and forth. Like the horses before him, he was bursting with good health.

"No Matty yet," James said, echoing Mandy's thoughts.

"No," she replied, half-dreading, half-longing to catch a glimpse of the gray mare. How many horses was that so far — four? Four more to go.

James tapped her on the arm. "See that man over there? He's bought all of Wilfred's horses up to now."

Mandy looked across at the man. She read the large card he held up to the auctioneer as he bought Treacle. "Newcombe," she read aloud. It wasn't a local name.

"Who is that, Dad?" she asked, when Dr. Adam paused for a minute near the barrier during a break in the bidding.

"Jim Newcombe," Dr. Adam answered. "He owns large riding stables near York. He's well-respected and takes excellent care of his horses."

"Oh." Mandy was relieved. At least Wilfred's horses would be well treated.

As the auction resumed, Dr. Adam went back over to the pens.

"And now, the fifth horse on sale today from Bennetts' stables," said the auctioneer over the loudspeaker. "Where will we start the bidding for Blaze — a handsome fifteen-year-old?"

Mandy tightened her fingers on the barrier. Just three more of Wilfred's horses to be sold: William, Honey, and Matty. Who would be next? Honey's name rang out and the sandy-colored mare lifted her head and whinnied as she was led around the ring. Then came the sound of the hammer hitting wood again. That was it.

"Two left now," Mandy breathed. Suddenly, her throat felt tight with unshed tears. It was almost over. She wondered what Wilfred was thinking.

"That Newcombe man bought Blaze and Honey as well," James said. "He must have tons of money."

"I hope he's got enough left to buy William and Matty, too," Mandy responded, crossing her fingers for luck. *I'll give Matty a final hug when I give her the apple*, she thought.

The loudspeaker crackled to life again. "And now the seventh and last of the horses from Bennetts' Stables. William is a nine-year-old gelding. . . ."

Mandy's eyes widened in surprise. That couldn't be right. William wasn't the *last* of Wilfred's horses. There was still Matty to come.

"Hey! What's going on?" said James.

"I don't know," Mandy replied.

They waited expectantly while William was led

around the sale ring. The auctioneer acknowledged the last few bids. "Any more? Do we have the last bid? Sold to Mr. Newcombe! That was the final horse from Bennetts' Stables. And now we have Bruce. A Shetland pony . . ."

Mandy looked at James. "But what about *Matty*?"

He shook his head, as surprised as she was.

Mandy was too stunned to react at first. Then worry began creeping in. Where could Matty be? Suddenly she knew what she must do: "I've got to find Wilfred," she said.

"But your dad told us to stay right here," James reminded her.

Mandy hesitated. Her dad's instructions had been clear and she didn't want to get into trouble, but she just had to find out what had happened to Matty.

"Look, Wilfred's just over there," she said, catching sight of the stooped figure. "I won't be long. I'll be back before Dad comes over here to get us."

Some of the buyers moved back to let her pass, but others glared down at her disapprovingly. Mandy bent and made herself as small as she could and squeezed her way through the crush of people.

It was a few minutes before she managed to get through the crowd. "Wilfred! Mr. Bennett!" she called in an urgent whisper.

She had to call twice more before Wilfred turned around. He looked dazed, as if he couldn't believe this was really happening.

"Oh, hello, Mandy. You shouldn't be over here, dear. It's a little too hectic around this area."

"Yes, I know," she said. "I'm going back in a minute. But I wanted to ask you . . . where's Matty? James and I have been watching out for her."

"Uh, Matty?" Wilfred's gaze slid sideways, then he took off his cap and began examining it intently.

"Yes. Has she been sold yet?" Surely he couldn't have forgotten about Matty!

"Oh, don't worry about Matty," Wilfred said, speaking rapidly in a low voice. "She's going to be fine."

But Mandy was worried. She couldn't explain it, even to herself, but she had a funny, anxious feeling. Something was going on, she just knew it.

"Didn't you bring Matty here with the other horses?" she persisted, having to raise her voice to be heard.

"Hush," Wilfred said, so low that she had to strain to hear him. Suddenly, he looked up, meeting her gaze as if he wanted to impress his words upon her. His faded blue eyes were still as bleak as they had been earlier, but now they shone with determination. "I told you," he said, "I've got other plans for Matty. You mustn't worry. Leave it be."

With that, Wilfred put his cap back on, then turned away and began making a path for himself through the people who were leading the horses toward the exit.

Puzzled, Mandy was about to hurry after Wilfred and ask him some more questions. But then, a deep voice beside her said, "Mandy!"

"Oh!" She almost jumped out of her skin. "Dad!"

"Who were you expecting?" Dr. Adam clapped a hand on his daughter's shoulder. "I thought I asked you and James to stay together! A busy auction is not a place to go wandering around."

"Yes, I know, Dad," Mandy began. "I'm sorry, but I just had to . . ."

Dr. Adam sighed. "Don't tell me. I know that look on your face. I might have known. Animals always come first with you. You're worried about Wilfred's horses, aren't you?"

Yes — she was worried, but only about one particular horse now — Matty. Mandy wanted to know what Wilfred had meant when he said he had "special plans" for the silver-gray mare. She sighed and nodded.

"Come on, Mandy," Dr. Adam said. "Let's get back to James. We're almost finished here anyway. Wilfred's horses all have a good home. We have to be content with that."

Mandy bit her lip and fell into step with her father. "But that's just it, Dad. Not all of Wilfred's horses have been sold today — what about Matty?"

Dr. Adam stroked his dark beard thoughtfully. "Now that you mention it, I don't recall checking her over with the other horses."

"Why don't you look at your list?" Mandy suggested. "If Matty was in the auction, her name will be on it."

"Good idea." Dr. Adam reached into his coat pocket and took out a crumpled piece of paper. He smoothed it out and scanned the columns of owners' and horses' names. After a few seconds he frowned. "You're right. Matty's name's not listed. How strange."

"I knew it!" Mandy said, though Matty's name being missing from her dad's list explained nothing.

Matty had to be somewhere. But where?

Two

"Are you going to Wilfred's house today?" Mandy asked her dad a couple of days after the horse sale. She was eager to hear how he was doing and, more particularly, to hear an explanation about Matty.

Adam Hope shook his head as he poured himself a cup of coffee. "I've been meaning to go and see him, but we've had a ton of emergencies. I was up at Greystones Farm all yesterday morning. Nelson, the Gills' boar, slipped in the mud and injured his leg."

The boar was a British Saddleback, very handsome with his spotted, black-and-white coloring and big floppy ears. He was also enormous, weighing about four hundred pounds.

"Poor Nelson," Mandy said. "Was the leg broken?"

"No," her dad replied. "It was a greenstick fracture: The bone was partly broken and partly bent. I put a cast on and gave him a sedative." He flashed her a grin. "Nelson didn't seem too grateful."

Emily Hope was buttering her toast. "There was another emergency at Baildon Farm. One of Jack Mabson's Jerseys had a nasty case of bloat."

"Which one?" Mandy asked worriedly. "Not Goldie, was it?"

Dr. Emily smiled. "No. The little calf is fine. It was Patsy. I gave her a bath of peanut oil in warm water and she was much better by the time I left. I'm going up to Baildon Farm today to check that she's okay."

"Oh," Mandy was relieved. It was certainly busy at Animal Ark. With her mom out on call and her dad in the clinic, it didn't look as if anyone would have time to check on Wilfred.

Mandy got up from the table and took her breakfast plate over to the sink. Her parents might not have time to visit Wilfred, but she and James did. "I'll just do my chores and look in on Bonny before I meet James," she said, making a dash for the door.

Bonny was a toy poodle who had been admitted with a badly cut foot. She was Mandy's favorite patient at the moment. Dr. Emily had suspected cut tendons, but she had operated and found the tendons undamaged. She had managed to repair the torn pads. Now Bonny was doing fine.

In the residential unit, Mandy mopped floors, cleaned out cages, and changed water dishes. The work wasn't very exciting, but it had to be done. She thought about Wilfred as she finished her chores. Maybe he'd feel more like talking about Matty today.

After washing her hands, she opened Bonny's cage. "Hello, girl," she said, taking the little dog out. "How are you feeling today?"

As Mandy stroked the tightly curled fur, Bonny gave a friendly whine and licked her on the chin. "You'll be going home soon," Mandy said. Bonny gave a soft woof, as if she understood everything Mandy said. *She probably does*, thought Mandy with a grin; poodles were very intelligent dogs.

Back in the Animal Ark reception area, Mandy glanced at the wall clock. It was almost time for morning office hours. *Time to go and meet James*, she thought and went to find her mom and dad to tell them she was leaving.

Adam Hope's voice floated out of the open examination room door. "I'm not surprised that Sam Western snapped up the old Bennett place," he was saying to his wife. "You have to hand it to that man, he knows a good thing when he sees it."

As Mandy walked into the room, Emily Hope nodded. "He's probably the only farmer around here wealthy enough to raise the money on short notice." She was taking packs of sterile dressing from a cabinet.

Mandy went over and held open the cabinet door to help her mom. "Thanks," Dr. Emily said. "Could you put a few of these over there?"

"Do you think Mr. Western will farm Wilfred's old land?" Mandy asked.

"I suppose he might," her dad said. "He's the type who always has an eye toward expansion. You can bet that he sees his new purchase strictly as a business proposition."

Everyone in Welford knew that Sam Western prided himself on having the most modern machinery in his milking sheds. He had annoyed quite a few people in the past with his pompous manner.

"We'll just have to wait and see, I suppose," Dr. Emily said, going to the sink to wash her hands with antibacterial soap. "No sense in worrying about it."

Dr. Adam half-turned away and sneaked a snack-sized chocolate bar from his coat pocket. Mandy eyed the chocolate bar. So much for his latest diet.

"Dad! That's millions of calories. How could you? And right after breakfast, too."

"It's only a tiny one, hardly more than a cookie," Dr. Adam said, innocently raising his eyebrows until they almost disappeared into his dark hair. "Besides, a little junk food now and then gives the old immune system a boost."

"Oh, right." Mandy made a face, unconvinced. She glanced at her mom and rolled her eyes.

Dr. Emily returned the look. "He'll be out jogging up toward the Beacon this weekend, trying to run the calories off! I hope you're ready to go with him on yet another training session."

"That's it, you two! Gang up on me." Adam Hope affected a hurt expression, but his eyes gleamed with good humor. He popped the last of the chocolate into his mouth and chewed defiantly. "Delicious!"

Just then Jean Knox, Animal Ark's receptionist, popped her head around the door. "Ready for this morning's first patient?" she inquired cheerily.

"I'd better go." Mandy made a lunge for the door. "I've got to meet James. Bye, Mom. Bye, Dad. See you later."

Flying out of Animal Ark, she took her bike from the shed and pedaled briskly down the narrow street. James was waiting for her by the bus stop outside the Fox and Goose restaurant.

"Oh, you brought Blackie with you!" Mandy laid her bike on the grass at the side of the road and knelt down to stroke the labrador's floppy ears.

Blackie wriggled his body and wagged his thick tail. He pushed his cold wet nose into Mandy's hand, inviting her to pet him more.

"Ow!" James complained as the dog's tail thwacked against his jeans. "That stings."

Mandy chuckled. "Well, you should know to get out of the way by now!" Blackie's manners had never been very good and they didn't seem to be improving with age.

"Did your dad call and ask Wilfred about Matty?" asked James.

Mandy shook her head. "He's been too busy to go and see him. I thought we could go."

"Fine with me," James said, getting on his bike.

They pedaled along the hilly road toward the out-skirts of Welford, easing into a lower gear to tackle the steep hills. Soon they rounded a curve in the road and saw Wilfred's house ahead of them.

"Wow!" James leaned forward on his handlebars and blew a silent whistle. "Just look at that!"

"Oh!" Mandy stopped quickly in a pile of pebbles, al-most falling off her bike in amazement.

A high wooden fence had been put up between the house and what was now Sam Western's land, cutting off Wilfred's view of his old stables. It looked very imposing.

"Huh! Someone's been busy!" Mandy said disapprovingly.

"Yeah. And we don't need three guesses to figure out who!" muttered James.

From beyond the new fence came the sounds of hammering and sawing.

"What do you think's happening over there?" asked James.

Mandy shrugged. "I don't know. Maybe Wilfred does, though. We could ask him."

"Come on," said James.

They leaned their bikes against the new fence, then knocked on the front door. There was no answer. Mandy picked up the horse-shaped knocker and gave three decisive raps. Still nothing. She bent forward and put her ear to the door.

"I can't hear anything."

"I'm not surprised, with that noise coming through the fence," said James. "Maybe Wilfred's out shopping."

"Let's check in the back," Mandy said. "Maybe he left the back door open."

But the back door was firmly closed and the yard, a tiny square of concrete hardly big enough to hold the garbage can, was also empty. Mandy noticed that the curtains were closed in the back sitting room.

"That's funny," she said.

James frowned. "What is?"

Mandy pointed to the window. "Look. Why would Wilfred close the curtains in the daytime?"

James agreed that it seemed strange. Mandy knocked on the back door, but there was still no answer. After a minute or so, she and James walked back around to the front of the house.

Mandy lifted the knocker again. "Let's give it one last try."

From the corner of her eye, she thought she saw some movement at a downstairs window. "He's in there, I'm sure of it."

"Mr. Bennett! Wilfred!" she and James chorused. "It's us, Mandy Hope and James Hunter."

There was a long pause, then they heard a bolt being unlatched inside the front door. The door opened a crack and Wilfred Bennett peered out worriedly from the dark interior. When he saw that they were alone, his wrinkled old face relaxed.

"Hello, you two," he said, sounding relieved.

"Hi, Wilfred. We came to see how you are," Mandy said. "We thought you weren't in."

"I'm not in for most people," Wilfred said quietly. "I don't want to be bothered, you see. I'm best left alone."

James reddened. "Sorry. We . . . um . . . just wanted to ask you about Matty," he said awkwardly.

Wilfred scratched his head, so that his straggly white hair stuck up in fluffy tufts. He looked flustered. "Okay — well, thanks for coming. I'm fine, really."

"And Matty?" Mandy coaxed, when it looked as if Wilfred wasn't going to mention her. "You said you had plans for her."

A panicked expression flickered across Wilfred's face. "Did I?"

"Yes," Mandy said. "You did." She was worried. There was something different about Wilfred. He seemed jumpy and on edge.

"Dear me, now. I'm getting so forgetful." Wilfred played with the buttons on his cardigan. "Well, anyway," he said vaguely. "Like I already told you, Matty's fine."

There was an awkward silence, broken by a soft "woof" from Blackie, who was behaving himself for once. He sat next to James, his tail thumping in a friendly fashion, a doggy grin stretching from ear to ear.

A smile flickered across Wilfred's tired face. *For a moment*, Mandy thought, *he looked like his old self*.

"Now then, boy." Wilfred patted the labrador's broad, dark head, smiling at James. "He's a great young dog."

"Wilfred," Mandy began, encouraged to have one more try. "About Matty . . ."

Wilfred's face closed down like a shutter. "Well — I've got to go inside now," he said quickly. "I've . . . uh . . . got something cooking on the stove. Say hello to your mom and dad for me, Mandy."

Before Mandy and James could say another word, Wilfred had closed the door, quick as a flash.

"Oh." Mandy heard the sound of bolts being shut and locks turned. How strange. She had been to the house many times and the doors had never even been locked, let alone bolted.

James also looked puzzled. "Did you smell anything cooking?"

"No, I didn't," Mandy said, still worried. "Wilfred was acting strangely, wasn't he?"

James nodded, then he shrugged. "Maybe it upsets him to talk about Matty," he suggested reasonably.

That could be it, Mandy thought. Poor Wilfred. But in the back of her mind there was still doubt. Something was wrong.

"Come on," James said.

"Okay," Mandy replied. "There's no point in hanging around here."

Blackie followed obediently as they retraced their steps and got their bikes. Mandy glanced over her shoulder and thought she saw the curtain at the kitchen window twitch.

"Wilfred's watching, making sure that we leave," she said to James.

"But why would he do that?"

"I wish I knew," Mandy said, wheeling her bike onto the road and scooting along with one foot on the pedal.

They moved a few yards along the road, to where they could see into the field. Over the hedge, they had a clear view of Wilfred's old yard and stable buildings.

"Sam Western hasn't knocked them down," said James. "I thought he would."

"He might still," Mandy said, noticing the car and builder's van parked outside the stable block.

Suddenly, Blackie barked and leaped forward. He'd seen a rabbit. James tried to grab his collar, but it was too late. The labrador shot through the nearby open gate and ran across the field toward the stable block.

"Oh, no!" Mandy gasped. It was just like Blackie. He only had to see the white tail of a rabbit and he was off.

James pedaled after Blackie in a fury, his body bent over the handlebars. "Quick! We have to catch him."

There's not much chance of that, thought Mandy. The young labrador was stocky like all his breed, but he could run like a greyhound when he put his mind to it.

"Hang on a sec!" she called, fumbling with her bike in her haste. But James was already halfway to the old yard; there was nothing to do but follow him.

Outside the stable, there was a muscular workman in overalls, whom neither of them recognized as a local. He watched Mandy and James approach, an amused look on his pleasant face. He pointed toward Blackie, who was now little more than a speck in the distance, and called out jauntily, "He went thataway!"

Next to the workman was a second man, who was leaning against a car. Mandy recognized the stern, sharp features at once. It was Dennis Saville, Sam Western's farm manager.

"Uh-oh," she murmured.

James slowed down. He turned to wait for Mandy to catch up. "Do you see who that is?"

Mandy nodded.

Mandy and James had clashed with Dennis Saville before. They knew him to be a humorless, matter-of-fact type who was only concerned with following his boss's orders.

"I suppose you realize you're trespassing," Dennis Saville said, frowning, as he walked toward Mandy and James.

James reddened. "We didn't mean to," he said. "We're just trying to catch my dog."

"Obviously," said Dennis Saville coldly. "I suggest you call it to heel."

There's a fat chance of Blackie taking any notice, Mandy thought. She felt embarrassed for James, who could only wait helplessly until Blackie got bored and trotted back by himself.

Luckily, at that moment, Blackie did just that. Having lost the scent of the rabbit, he came panting down the field toward them, curious to know what was going on. He went straight up to Dennis Saville, his tail wagging, beaming one of his silly doggy grins.

Mandy groaned, sensing trouble.

Anybody else would have pet the friendly dog, but not Dennis Saville. "You'd better put that dog on a leash," he said sternly, "if you can't control it."

Mandy knew that James must be dying to say that Blackie was not an "it."

Red to his ears, James got off his bike, put a collar on Blackie, and clipped on the leash, saying, "His name's Blackie." Lowering his voice so that only Mandy could hear, he added, "You should know that! You've met him before."

"I don't care what its name is," Dennis Saville replied. Then, turning to Mandy, he said, "What are you doing out here, anyway? You're the vets' daughter, aren't you?"

While Mandy nodded, James glared at the man in silence.

"We came to visit Wilfred," Mandy explained. "He's our friend."

Dennis Saville nodded. "I remember him telling my boss that you kids helped him out with the horses when his wife was ill in the hospital. Well, this place won't be used as stables anymore."

"What's it going to be used for, then?" James asked, curiosity triumphing over his anger.

At first, Mandy thought Dennis Saville wasn't going to reply. It would be just like him to tell James to mind his own business. The big man in overalls, who had been watching in silence until now, winked at Mandy and James, then spoke to Dennis Saville.

"I'm putting the sign up later," he said mildly. "Everybody will soon know about your boss turning the field into a campsite."

"A campsite?" Mandy whispered, looking at James.

Dennis Saville glanced sharply at the burly workman. He looked as if he might be about to tell the man not to interfere, then he shrugged.

"Show them what you've been doing, if you like," he said. "But don't waste too much time. I've got business to attend to. I'll be back later."

Silently, James mouthed, "Wow!"

Mandy was speechless. Wonders would never cease; Dennis was being almost human for once.

Dennis Saville strode over to his car and got in. "Just a quick look inside," he said from the open window. "And tie that dog up outside."

"Okay," said James, too surprised even to feel angry anymore.

As Dennis Saville's car disappeared through the open gate, the workman reached down to pet Blackie. "Hello, boy. You're a friendly one, aren't you?" He gave a small toss of his head in the direction of the gate. "Not much of a dog lover, that Dennis Saville, is he?"

"He likes Sam Western's nasty bulldogs all right!" said James. "They're horrible."

"It's not the bulldogs' fault." Mandy couldn't help speaking up. She loved all animals and knew that if dogs were wary and hostile, then usually the owners were at fault. "Sam Western's trained them to be that way."

"That's true," James admitted.

Once inside the stable block, Mandy and James stared in amazement. The place smelled of new paint and sawdust. The workman had been busy painting the ceiling and walls white. Six of the eight stalls had been fitted with doors, and against one wall there were two tiled sinks with mirrors above them.

"What do you think?" the workman said. "It makes a good bathroom, doesn't it?"

"Yes," Mandy agreed politely. "Very nice."

She looked wistfully at the two stalls that had been left empty. Not long ago she and James had been mucking them out, spreading fresh new bedding, and filling hay nets for Wilfred's horses. Instead of fresh paint and the noise of hammering, there had been the sounds of horses shifting contentedly in their stalls and the smell of saddle soap and hoof oil.

And, best of all, there had been the feel of Matty's soft mouth as she had gently taken the crunchy, red apple from Mandy's hand.

Three

The following morning, Mandy was helping her dad treat a baby hedgehog with an infected foot. Betty Hilder, who ran the local animal shelter, had brought the little animal into Animal Ark. It was part of a litter that had been found in a barn, after the mother was killed on the road.

"Yes," Betty was saying, "I saw definite signs of badgers in the woods in back of Wilfred Bennett's old place. I was planning to release two rescued hedgehogs up there, Susie and Tess. But I've changed my mind now."

"Lucky for Susie and Tess!" Dr. Adam said. "Badgers

are one of the few animals capable of tackling a hedge-hog."

"Exactly," Betty said. "I'm happy to see badgers moving back into the woods, but I'm going to have to find somewhere else to release my hedgehogs."

"Wouldn't it be wonderful if a whole colony of badgers moved in?" Mandy said, her eyes shining. She held the hedgehog gently but firmly as Dr. Adam tipped antibiotic powder onto the cleaned foot.

"A whole cete of them would be even better," her dad replied.

"Dad! That's the same thing as a colony!"

Dr. Adam gave her one of his lopsided smiles. "Just testing," he said.

Betty Hilder chuckled. "You can't trick Mandy! How's little Midge doing? Will she need to stay here?"

"What a great name! It really suits her," Mandy said. Midge made snuffling noises and her pointed nose wrinkled as she sniffed at the air. Her spines were still faintly pink and very soft. "She's so tiny."

"Compared to Susie and Tess, she is," Betty agreed. "Those two are a couple of bruisers! It's hard to believe they were this small when they came to me."

Dr. Adam smiled. "I think you can take Midge back to the shelter. She's thriving on being hand-fed. If you're at all worried about that foot, give me a call."

"Thanks. I will." Betty picked Midge up and put her back into a straw-lined box. Almost before Betty Hilder was out the door, Mandy had shrugged off her white lab coat. Washing his hands at the sink beside her, Dr. Adam smiled. "Thanks for your help. I don't need three guesses to know where you're off to now." His dark eyes twinkled. "Nice day for a walk in the woods!"

Mandy flashed her dad a grin as she left the examination room. If a badger family *had* moved back into the woods, she definitely wanted to know about it.

"Wow!" said James, when Mandy told him. "Let's go up there right now."

Mandy grinned. "I thought you'd say that. What about Blackie?"

"Not a good idea!" said James. "Dogs and badgers don't mix very well!"

He looked thoughtful. Mandy knew that he hated leaving Blackie behind.

James's face brightened. "I just remembered. Mom's got a friend coming over who always brings Blackie's favorite dog biscuits. I don't think he'll mind staying at home — just this once!"

The sun shone brightly as they pedaled through the town of Welford. At the edge of the woods, they took one of the bridle paths that snaked through the trees.

After a spell of wet weather, the woods were ablaze with many shades of green.

"This is near the place," Mandy said after a while. "We have to leave the bikes here."

They made their way up the hillside on foot. Dappled light flickered through the trees and the rich smell of wet leaves rose from beneath their feet.

"This seems like a good lookout spot," whispered James, crouching down behind a tangle of branches. "Let's use these bushes for cover."

"Yes," Mandy agreed, dropping down beside him. She felt like a commando as she squirmed forward, using her elbows and knees.

She peered through the bushes. Directly in front of her, the ground dipped sharply to a hollow. Beneath twisted tree roots and the yellowing stalks of bluebells and primroses, the slopes were honeycombed with entrances to disused tunnels.

"I don't think we'll see any badgers," whispered James. "Even though they sometimes come out in the daytime."

"No," Mandy said, craning her neck. "I bet they're safe underground, all curled up in their grassy nests." It sounded cozy, but she knew badgers faced many dangers from humans and dogs.

James squinted against the sun, which was reflecting

off his glasses. He put up a hand to shade his face. "Did Betty say she definitely saw signs of digging? I can't see a thing."

"I can!" Mandy whispered excitedly, tugging at his arm. "Move over here a little. See?" She pointed to a pile of sandy earth outside a hole halfway up the slope. "It's a freshly turned pile of dirt! Betty's right. New badgers have moved in."

"Wow!" said James, settling his glasses more firmly on his nose. "Isn't it great? I wonder if it's a sow. There might be cubs, too."

Mandy felt excited. "I hope so. They're really smart. They've got ready-made homes in those deserted burrows and lots of food."

James nodded. "That leaf pile looks inches deep. I bet it's just teeming with juicy worms and beetles and stuff."

"Yeah!" Mandy said with a grin. "Sounds like badger heaven!" Suddenly she was serious. "We'll have to be really careful who we tell about this. Dad and Betty know already, of course, but they won't tell anyone else."

"Right," agreed James, his brows drawn together in a fierce frown. "It'll be our secret. No one's going to hurt these badgers. Not if we have anything to say about it!"

Mandy felt a shiver run down her back. They had

once encountered a group of badger hunters, and it still horrified her to think of the poor badgers in danger.

"I can't understand why anyone thinks it's fun to hurt an animal," she said angrily. "It's so cruel. I hate all kinds of hunting."

"Me, too," said James. "It's a good thing that lots of people agree with us. Most of them really care about animals."

"That's true," Mandy said, cheering up as they crept quietly back to the path where they had left their bikes. She cared a great deal. That's why she wanted to be a vet like her mom and dad when she was older.

They pedaled slowly back along the bridle path, enjoying the warmth of the sun on their backs. Mandy found her thoughts dwelling on Matty. She really missed the elderly little mare. She wondered who owned her now. They were so near Wilfred's house that she couldn't resist the temptation to stop by and visit him.

"Should we bike back past the Bennetts' old field?" she suggested casually. "We might catch a glimpse of Wilfred. Sometimes he sits in the doorway of his house, enjoying the sun."

She saw that James wasn't fooled one bit. "Don't tell me. You want another chance to ask him about Matty."

"Yup. That's my idea." Mandy glanced at her friend.

James was wearing his serious look. "What's wrong? Do you think I'm making too much of a big deal about Matty?"

"No," James said heatedly, reddening under her direct gaze. "Okay, then, maybe a little," he admitted. "I told my dad about the auction and Matty not being there and he said Wilfred must have sold Matty privately."

"I guess he did," Mandy agreed, thinking that James's logical explanation still didn't explain why Wilfred was acting so mysteriously. "I want to know who bought Matty. That's all. If her new owner's not too far away, we might be able to go and visit her."

James grinned. "Well — you do still owe her a red apple!"

Mandy couldn't help smiling. That was true.

"It's not just Matty. It's Wilfred," she said after a moment. "He seem so different somehow. Not just sad and quiet like he has been, but anxious about something."

She couldn't explain it, even to herself. Wilfred had been so flustered and worried-looking when they visited him a couple of days ago. It just wasn't like him.

James scooted forward and pedaled out from under the trees. "Come on. I don't mind going that way. I want to see what's going on up at the new campsite anyway."

Mandy knew that James was concerned about Wilfred, too, although he hid it better than she did. They pedaled fast down the path to the road, then coasted down the hills. As they approached the outskirts of the town, they saw the new wooden fence. Wilfred's house, only a few yards away from the high fence, looked somehow isolated and cut off.

"Isn't it awful?" Mandy murmured. "All Wilfred has in the world now is his house. Instead of green fields and horses, he has a boring view of the road."

"Hey! Look at that," said James, pointing to the new sign, which read WESTERN'S CAMPSITE in bold letters. "Anybody would think the place was a vacation site instead of an almost bare field."

It was typical of the pompous landowner, Mandy thought. "Look. The gate's open and there are people in the field."

Stakes had been hammered into the ground to mark out tent pitches. Mandy and James leaned forward on their handlebars and watched the campers putting up their tents.

"Look at that one. It's like a house," said James.

In one corner, a trailer tent was slowly being transformed into a multiroomed canvas bungalow, complete with floor-length picture windows, canopy, and porch. Two adults and two children were unloading a great deal of equipment from a car. There were airbeds, sleeping bags, hang-up wardrobes, and even a cooker. You name it, these campers had it.

Mandy expected them to unpack a full-size bath at any moment. "Look. That tent's just the opposite!" she said.

Just inside the gate, a tall, thin woman, wearing a bright red beret, baggy army shorts, and walking boots, was putting up a low, green tent. Her movements were quick and efficient as she slung a fly-sheet over her tent and began pegging it down. An enormous bulging backpack lay on the grass, and running around it excitedly was a brown-and-white Jack Russell terrier.

"Sparky, calm down," the woman said mildly. The little dog promptly sat. He watched, ears pricked intelligently, as his owner finished pitching the tent. "That's better. You know I insist on good manners."

"What an obedient dog," said James with a trace of longing in his voice.

Mandy knew he was wishing Blackie took the slightest notice of anything he was told. "Don't feel bad," she said. "Blackie understands a few words."

"Yeah, two of them! 'Walk' and 'Food'!" James said.

The woman looked up and saw Mandy and James watching. "Hello there!" she called cheerily. "Do you live in town?"

Mandy nodded. "I'm Mandy Hope; my mom and dad

are vets in Welford. This is James Hunter, my best friend."

As Mandy and James wandered over, the woman gave a broad grin. "How do you do," she said, shaking hands with each of them. "I'm Flora Pearson and this is Sparky."

The formal introduction and old-fashioned handshake amused Mandy and she grinned back.

"Pleased to meet you, Sparky," she said, bending down to pet the little dog. The Jack Russell's long tail wagged as he rolled on his back, his tongue lolling in a wide grin.

"Really, Sparky! Have you no shame?" Flora said, her eyes sparkling with good humor. "He thrives on attention."

Mandy chuckled. "What a friendly little dog!"

"Oh, Sparky loves everyone and everything. Except for horses. He's a terror around them. I have to call him to heel, otherwise he goes after them like a shot, barking and making tons of noise!"

"He'll be fine here," Mandy said. "There were riding stables here once, but not anymore. And it's mainly sheep up on the hills."

"Oh. Sparky has nothing against wool sweaters!" Flora joked.

Mandy and James laughed with her. "Do you need any help with your tent?" asked James politely.

"How kind of you to ask," Flora said. "But I've just about finished. I was going to make some iced tea. Would you like to join me? We so enjoy having visitors, don't we, Sparky?"

Sparky tilted his head and rolled his lips back. He sat up very straight, with all his teeth showing, his eyes wide in a glassy stare.

"Yikes!" James said, not sure what to make of the little dog. "What's wrong with him?"

"Oh, that's just Sparky's way of smiling," Flora explained. "Some people are a bit alarmed when he first does that."

Mandy wasn't surprised. She laughed. "Did you teach him that?"

Flora shook her head. "Oh, no. Sparky did it all by himself. He's very intelligent."

Mandy and James sprawled on the grass outside Flora's tent while she spooned iced tea mix into a huge pitcher. Mandy looked across at James. No wonder the backpack was bulging if Flora carried all this around with her.

Mandy hid a smile. Flora Pearson was somewhat strange, but in a nice way. After a minute or two, Flora rummaged through the backpack and brought out another square tin and four brightly patterned tin mugs. She poured iced tea into three of them, and water into the fourth.

James frowned. "Four?" he mouthed silently at Mandy.

"There you are, Sparky. That's yours," Flora said. She smiled at Mandy and James. "He always has the yellow mug."

Mandy and James burst out laughing as the little dog placed one paw on either side of the mug, dipped his head, and delicately lapped his water.

"Brownie, anyone?" Flora said, opening the square tin. "I made them myself. Sparky won't eat store-bought cakes."

Of course he won't, Mandy thought. As they drank their iced tea and ate brownies, Flora explained that she was on a hiking trip.

"Sparky and I are just staying here for the night," she said. "Tomorrow we're off to explore the hills up past the Beacon."

"It's beautiful up there," Mandy said. She knew the area well. Her dad often went jogging up there. "Wonderful views across the valleys."

Flora seemed pleased to have found someone with

knowledge of the area. She spread a battered map on the grass. Smoothing out the creases, she traced the long slope up to the hills with a thin finger. "We'll start here, bright and early."

"Oh, look. There's Upper Welford Hall. Sam Western owns it. He's a local farmer," Mandy said. "He owns this campsite, too."

"Really? Do you know everyone around here?" Flora said.

"She should," James said. "Her mom and dad visit all the farms, even the isolated ones up there."

Flora gave a delighted laugh. "Do you hear that, Sparky? We've just met local celebrities!"

Mandy and James looked at each other. They'd never been called celebrities before. "We're not famous," Mandy giggled, liking Flora more by the minute. "But my friend's mom is. She plays the parson's wife in *Parson's Close*." It was her grandma's favorite soap opera on TV.

"Wow!" Flora said. "Sparky loves watching TV."

Mandy and James exchanged a glance. Of course he did!

After they finished their drinks, they offered to fill Flora's water container. "So kind," Flora said, handing them what looked like a sturdy, rolled-up plastic bag fixed to a coat hanger. Flora's water storage container was as eccentric as the woman herself!

Sparky scampered up the field with them to the tap outside the old stable block. He sat, head to one side, watching as water gushed into the container, making it swell into a potbellied shape. Then he walked beside them back down the field, trotting obediently at their feet.

"Good boy," said James, looking down at the little dog. He smiled across at Mandy. "I think he's guarding Flora's homemade water carrier. As if anyone would want to steal it!"

"Thanks," Flora said upon their return. She hung the container from a low tree branch in the shade, where there was a strange object already hanging from a hook.

"What's that thing?" whispered James, eyeing the contraption that seemed to be a tube made of wire and old net curtain. It was gathered at the top and bottom and there was a plastic plate in the base.

"I think it's a food safe," Mandy said. "It keeps food cool and stops flies from getting into it. I saw instructions on how to make one in an old Girl Scout book of Mom's."

"I didn't know people still made stuff like that," said James.

"It looks like Flora does!"

Half an hour later, James jumped up. He and Mandy had been enjoying throwing a hard rubber ball for Sparky. "What time is it? I just remembered I've got to get back early. Mom's visitor's staying for dinner." He looked really guilty.

"Oh, dear," Flora said, looking concerned. "Have Sparky and I kept you from something important?"

"No. I mean yes. Well — sort of," James stammered, blushing. "But it's not your fault."

Mandy turned to James. "It isn't very late. If we leave right now and get a move on, we'll get to your house in plenty of time."

"Okay." James looked relieved.

As they reached the gate, they waved good-bye. "Bye, Flora. Thanks for the iced tea. Bye, Sparky." Flora was piling fruit into the food safe. She looked over her shoulder and waved back.

"See you again, I hope. I'll probably camp here on my way back in a few days' time." Abruptly, she turned away and crawled into the low opening of her tent. They heard her say, "Now, Sparky, where do you want your sleeping bag?"

"I bet she made Sparky's bed herself!" James said as they walked their bikes along the outside of the new fence. "Flora's really wacky, isn't she?"

"Wacky but nice," Mandy said firmly.

"That's what I meant!" James said with a chuckle. Mandy laughed, too.

They threw themselves onto their bikes. "Race you," James called, speeding out of the gate.

"Okay. You're on!" Mandy flew after him, down the side of the campsite fence.

As Wilfred's house whizzed by, Mandy glanced at it, tempted to slow down. But in that brief second, she saw that there was no sign of movement at the windows and the front door was firmly closed. No sign of Wilfred sunning himself in the doorway.

The little nagging feeling was still there inside her. Despite James's words earlier it wouldn't go away. Mandy's instincts still told her that something just wasn't right.

The sound of Dr. Adam's rich baritone voice echoed around the living room. He was singing hymns, rehearsing for choir practice. The smell of baked potatoes filled the house. Dinner would soon be ready, but Mandy wanted a word with her dad before they sat down to eat.

She slipped quietly in through the door and curled up on the sofa. The living room was cozy, with its low ceiling and wooden beams. Red patterned rugs covered the stone floor. In the winter, a log fire burned in the fireplace, but right now the space with filled by a copper bucket packed with flowers from Grandpa's garden.

Dr. Adam sang on, while Mandy leafed through an old copy of *The Dalesman*. He trailed off after a few minutes.

"Interesting read?" he said innocently.

Mandy grinned and put down the magazine. "Not really."

"Okay. What's bugging you?" her dad asked. "I know that look. You're plotting something."

Mandy told her dad about the events of the day. "We didn't see Wilfred," she explained. "I wondered if you'd mind calling him?"

"You're still worried about him, aren't you?"

She nodded. "He's just not himself, Dad."

"Of course he's not. His wife just died, Mandy," Adam Hope said gently.

Mandy bit her lip. "Yes, I know. Do you think that's why he won't talk about Matty?"

"Oh, Matty. Of course!" Her dad closed his songbook. "Okay, Mandy. I'll give Wilfred a call. I've been meaning to check that he's okay anyway."

"Thanks, Dad!" Mandy jumped up. "I'll go and help Mom with dinner."

A few minutes later, Dr. Adam came into the kitchen.

Mandy was grating cheese into a bowl. Her dad took a pinch of cheese and popped it into his mouth. Mandy paused, too impatient for news of Wilfred to scold him.

"Did you speak to Wilfred, Adam?" Emily Hope asked, putting out plates.

"Yes," Dr. Adam said. "He sounds fine, says he's coping well by himself."

"Did you ask him about Matty?" Mandy asked eagerly. "Is she settling in okay? Are her new owners nearby?"

"Whoa! One question at a time!" her dad replied with a grin. "I mentioned Matty. Wilfred said I shouldn't worry about her. Everything's fine. He said he'll explain next time he sees me."

"But what does that mean?" Mandy persisted.

"It means that this food is ready," her mom said firmly. "Would you bring that bowl of salad over, please, Mandy?"

As she took her place at the table, Mandy was thoughtful. She seemed to be the only one who thought there was something strange about this whole thing. Could she be wrong? As she cut open a baked potato and mashed butter into it, she caught her dad's eye.

"Don't worry, sweetheart," Dr. Adam said. "It's understandable that Wilfred wants to be left alone after what he's been through."

"Yes," Dr. Emily agreed. "And we must respect his wishes, Mandy. All right?"

"All right," Mandy said reluctantly. But it wasn't all right. And it wouldn't be until she knew for sure where Matty was.

Four

Emily Hope popped a worming tablet into a small envelope. "If you're going to Grandma and Grandpa's, you may as well take this for Smoky," she said to Mandy.

Smoky was Mandy's grandma and grandpa's adopted cat.

"Okay," Mandy said, slipping the envelope into her jeans pocket.

Her mom wore a dark green suit with a cream blouse underneath, and her red hair was tied back. She was speaking at a veterinary conference near York and staying for the dinner afterward.

"You look really nice, Mom. I hope the talk goes well."

As Dr. Emily smiled, the freckles seemed to dance on her cheeks. "Thanks, honey. That sounds like my ride." She reached for her handbag and folder. "See you later."

"Bye!" Mandy called.

Saturdays were short working days at the clinic. With her mom out all day, Simon, the nurse, would be helping her dad with the office visits. Dr. Adam would be doing house calls after that. Simon was just arriving as Mandy closed the front door behind her: a tall, thin figure, with freshly cut blond hair and glasses. He raised his hand in a wave.

Most of the school vacation was gone already, Mandy thought as she walked up the road. She felt restless and a little edgy. If only she knew where Matty was. Thoughts of the little silver-gray mare continued to bother her, but since no one else seemed concerned she had decided to keep her worries to herself.

She sighed and told herself that a visit to her grandparents was just what she needed. There was always something going on at Lilac Cottage.

Just then, she saw her dad returning to Animal Ark in the Land Rover. He had been out to Woodbridge Farm Park on Walton Road.

Dr. Adam pulled up at the side of the road and leaned

across to the open window. "Hello there. Where are you off to?"

"I'm meeting James and Blackie at Grandma's," she replied. "We thought we might help out in the garden."

"That's really nice of you. Your grandpa swears that weeds grow overnight at this time of year," Dr. Adam chuckled. "But I'm not sure that Blackie and the word *help* go together!"

Mandy smiled. "Was there a serious problem at the Farm Park, Dad?"

"No. Just routine shots, then Mr. Marsh asked me to check over four new arrivals."

"What were they?" Mandy asked. "Anything interesting?"

"I thought all animals were interesting to you!"

"Of course they are! You know what I mean."

He nodded, his mild blue eyes teasing. "Actually — these *are* a little unusual. Mr. Marsh thinks his customers might find them interesting. They're Soay sheep, four of them."

"Oh. What are they like?"

"Small, brownish, with tiny little horns," Dr. Adam said. "They're an old breed, very tough and pretty rare."

"They sound great," Mandy breathed. "Can I go and see them sometime?"

Her dad flashed her a grin. "Now, how did I know you

were going to say that? I've got to go back there in a day or two. You can come with me, if you want to."

"Great!"

He drove the Land Rover forward. "Got to go and see a man about a dog! Bye! Say hello to your grandma and grandpa for me."

Mandy waved. "I will!" she called, as she continued on up the road.

She reached the gate, with its Lilac Cottage sign, just as James arrived. His head appeared, bobbing over the top of the neatly trimmed hedges.

"Hi, James. Hi, Blackie."

The labrador gave a friendly woof and wagged his tail as Mandy patted his head.

The bushes that gave the cottage its name were in full bloom, and a strong sweet scent hung in the air. Mandy and James had reached the front door, when they caught sight of something in the camper parked in the driveway.

First a hand appeared, scrubbing briskly away at the window with a piece of damp, crumpled newspaper. Then a face, topped by neat gray hair, came into view.

"Hi, Grandma!" Mandy waved.

Her grandma waved back. She was wearing a checkered apron and bright pink rubber gloves — just like an ad for dishwashing liquid.

"What's she doing with that newspaper?" asked James.

"It's probably one of her shortcuts," Mandy replied. Her grandma was a wealth of information about such things. "She says she's going to write a book one day — called, '1001 Things to Do Around the House with Vinegar,'" Mandy said.

"Vinegar! Was she joking?"

Mandy grinned. "Probably, but I'm not sure!"

James shook his head in disbelief, his dark hair flopping around. "She would get along well with Flora Pearson!"

"Mandy, dear!" Grandma's face lit up as she came out of the camper to meet them. She placed a plastic bowl on the ground. It was full of cleaning things: dust cloths, polish, scouring pads — and a bottle of vinegar. "How's my favorite granddaughter?"

Mandy almost exploded with laughter as she saw James looking suspiciously at the bottle of vinegar. "Your *only* granddaughter is fine, thanks very much!" she managed to say.

"Hello, James." Mrs. Hope's wide smile shone on James, too. Stripping off the apron and rubber gloves, she bent to give Blackie a pat.

"Hello, Mrs. Hope," said James.

Mandy took the small envelope out of her pocket. "Mom sent you this, for Smoky."

"Thanks, sweetheart." Grandma put the worming tablet in her dress pocket.

"You look busy," Mandy said. "Are you spring-cleaning the camper?"

Grandma's eyes twinkled. "You could call it that."

"What do you mean?" asked Mandy, puzzled.

"I've been keeping out of the way."

"Why?" Mandy asked.

"Come over here and see," Grandma said mysteriously.

Mandy, James, and Blackie wandered across to the garden. There were fruit trees and shrubs, rows of peas and beans, bushy potato plants on top of ridges, and brightly colored flowers bursting from their beds. Every inch of soil had something planted. Nothing could resist Grandpa's green thumb.

The greenhouse reached back to the garden fence. In the narrow space behind it, they saw Mandy's grandpa and a small man with frizzy whitish hair. Both men had a firm hold on the same panel of fencing.

"That's Ernie Bell with Grandpa," Mandy said, surprised.

Ernie Bell was a retired carpenter. He lived in a tiny house behind the Fox and Goose restaurant. He was grumpy and stubborn, but Mandy knew that his unfriendly scowl hid a good heart.

Grandma nodded, looking pleased with herself. "Yes. Your grandpa was struggling with taking down that damaged fence panel when Ernie just happened to call and offer to help."

Mandy chuckled, "Oh, he did, did he? What have you been up to, Grandma?"

Grandma smiled and reached up to sweep some stray hairs back into the braid at the back of her head. "I only mentioned to Ernie that your grandpa couldn't really manage the fence alone. I told him that he needed help with fixing it, but was too proud to ask."

"Grandma! You are awful," Mandy said.

"I know. But it worked. Ernie couldn't resist coming over to have a look, being a retired carpenter. I knew he'd be dying to lend a hand, but you can't just ask him. You have to know how to handle him."

Mandy nodded. "We know! He loves helping, but he has to do things his own way."

"Like when he made that pen for Lucky," added James. Lucky was a little fox cub Mandy and James had once rescued.

"But why have you been keeping out of the way in the camper?" Mandy asked.

Grandma gave another one of her twinkling grins. "Ernie's getting wise to my tricks. I thought I'd let your

Grandpa handle things this time. Just look at him! How do you think he's doing?"

Grandpa and Ernie seemed to be doing some kind of silly dance. They were jigging back and forth, pulling at the fence, and bending to get a better grip. Then they stopped altogether and stood back to take a look. Grandpa scratched his head. Ernie Bell rubbed the gray whiskers on his chin.

"I only hope Ernie doesn't keep calling your grandpa 'young Tom,'" whispered Grandma.

Mandy, James, and Grandma stood there watching. Next to Ernie, Mandy's grandpa looked tall and straight. At sixty-five, he was as fit as a fiddle. He was always on the go, always gardening, walking, or biking.

"Oh, no. I seem to be making a mess of this," Grandpa said. "It's a good thing you're here, Ernie."

Good for you, Grandpa, Mandy thought.

"Out of the way," Ernie said, taking charge. "Let me look at it."

Grandpa moved aside.

"Now then, young Tom. Grab a hold," Ernie ordered. "That's it. Give it a push and it'll come free of those rusty nails."

"You're right," Grandpa said meekly, on his best behavior. "You're the expert, the best retired carpenter in Yorkshire. There's no one better."

Mandy cringed. *Don't overdo it, Grandpa!*

Ernie frowned. "Humph! I don't know about that," he muttered grumpily, but he looked pleased.

Mandy breathed a sigh of relief. Ernie was falling for it.

"Now," Ernie said. "One, two, three — lift!"

With a final heave and a screech of metal, the fence panel came loose. Grandpa and Ernie moved sideways. Moments later, the damaged panel was propped against the wooden post.

"Phew!" Grandpa dusted off his hands. He looked up and waved. "Hello there. We seem to have attracted quite an audience!"

Mandy and James waved back. "Hi, Grandpa," called Mandy. "Hello, Mr. Bell! How's Sammy?"

"He's fine, thanks." Ernie Bell's wrinkled, weather-beaten face relaxed into a grin. "Bright-eyed and bushy-tailed!" He could never resist talking about his pet squirrel. He had brought Sammy into Animal Ark after the squirrel's mother was run over.

"Lunch is in five minutes," Grandma said.

"Great," Grandpa said, turning back to the fence panel.

The high winds of winter had torn ragged holes and splintered the wood. It was a complete mess. Mandy saw her grandpa scratch his head.

"Thanks for your help, Ernie. I guess I should try to patch this up now," he said doubtfully.

"Patch it up!" Ernie Bell's face wore a look of disgust. "I don't patch things up. I do a good job or I don't do it at all. Out of the way, Tom. Let me have a look." He reached in his pants pocket and took out a tape measure.

Grandpa moved nimbly aside. "You just tell me what I need and I'll go and get it from Fenton's lumberyard."

"No need for that," Ernie said, putting his head to one side. "I've got to pick up my tools. I'll get what we need on the way. Now, have you got any nails? It's important to have the right size."

Grandpa winked at Mandy as he and Ernie moved toward the small shed. She smiled back at him. *Great job!*

In the spotless kitchen, Grandma served sandwiches and poured glasses of homemade lemonade for Mandy and James. She had been baking that morning and the whole house smelled wonderful. On the table, there was a pie with a crispy latticework of pastry covering the fruit.

"Mmmm. What is it?" Mandy asked. "Apple and blackberries from your freezer?"

"Extra insurance!" Grandma said with a smile. "Just in case Ernie needed more persuading."

"Don't you mean bribing?" Mandy said.

"Mandy Hope!" Grandma teased. She cut thick slices and placed them on plates, then said to Mandy, "Would you get me the ice cream from the freezer, dear?"

Mandy washed her hands and helped Grandma dole out scoops of vanilla ice cream. Just then, Smoky came into the kitchen. Blackie walked up to the cat in a friendly fashion, his tail wagging back and forth.

Mandy bent down to pet the cat's silky gray fur. Smoky purred, winding around Mandy's legs. Then he sniffed her hand and began licking her fingers. Mandy giggled as the cat's warm, rough tongue tickled.

"It must be the ice cream!" said James. He chuckled. "I bet Sparky likes ice cream, too."

"I bet he even eats it with his own special spoon!" Mandy joked.

"Who's Sparky?" Grandma said suspiciously. "Not another of your new strays needing a good home?"

"Not this time!" Mandy said. "Sparky belongs to Flora Pearson, someone we met up at Western's Campsite." She and James filled her in on all the details about the eccentric woman and her quirky pet. "And Flora's coming back this way, so we'll probably get to see her and Sparky up at the campsite again," she finished.

Grandma smiled. "They sound like an interesting pair!"

"They are," James agreed.

"What's that?" Ernie Bell said, coming into the kitchen with Grandpa. On Grandma's invitation, he took a seat at the table. "Did somebody mention campers?"

Mandy nodded. "We were just telling Grandma about someone we met up at Western's Campsite the other day."

Ernie gave a dry chuckle that sounded like a rusty door creaking open. "Huh! Sam Western's not having things all his own way," he said. "There's been a bit of a to-do up there by all accounts."

"What sort of a to-do?" asked Grandpa.

But Ernie seemed in no hurry to share his juicy gossip. He sipped his lemonade and chewed slowly on a big piece of pie and ice cream.

"Another slice, Ernie?" Grandma asked sweetly.

"Don't mind if I do — if it's going to be leftover anyway," Ernie said, somehow managing to sound as if he was doing Grandma a favor.

Mandy and James were almost fidgeting with impatience. If something was going on up at the new campsite they definitely wanted to know about it! At long last, Ernie pushed his empty plate away. He looked around the table, enjoying having a captive audience.

"That campsite's haunted," he stated matter-of-factly.

Mandy and James blinked at him. Grandma looked

indignant. It was obvious that she didn't believe it — not for one minute. She opened her mouth to speak, but Grandpa laid a hand on her arm. "What makes you say that?" he asked mildly.

"It's not me saying it," Ernie said. "It's the campers. Well, according to Mrs. McFarlane."

"Mrs. McFarlane!" Grandma said with a sniff. "If a leaf fell in the woods that woman would hear it!"

Ernie looked annoyed. "Well, if you don't want to know what I've got say . . ." he said huffily, half-rising from the table.

"We want to know, don't we, James?" Mandy burst out.

James nodded.

"Go on, then, Ernie," Grandpa said. "Let's hear the rest of it."

Ernie sank back into his chair. "Well — as I heard it, a couple of campers went into the post office on their way out of Welford. They said they'd had just about enough and they'd decided to pack up and move on."

"But why?" asked Mandy.

"Because of the strange things going on," Ernie said darkly.

Mandy leaned forward eagerly, her blue eyes wide. "What sort of things?"

"Ghostly things," Ernie said, deadly serious. "People

have heard hoofbeats on the road beyond the fence. And" — he leaned forward, his face intent — "someone saw a headless horseman, riding by on a ghost horse."

Mandy's mouth dropped open. She looked across at James.

"That's nonsense!" Grandma said in her usual practical way. "I don't appreciate you frightening my granddaughter with these silly stories, Ernie Bell."

"Oh, it takes more than that to rattle Mandy," said Grandpa. "She's got a level head on her shoulders."

"You think they're just stories?" Ernie said, dropping his voice to a gruff whisper. "Then why is the campsite half-empty, huh? Tell me that. Something's definitely stopping people from camping up there."

"But a headless horseman?" Grandpa said reasonably.

Ernie looked a little sheepish. "Well — maybe not headless," he admitted. "But the rest of it's true. One of the campers told the McFarlanes how he looked out of his tent in the dead of night and he saw it — the outline of a man on a horse. "It was all misty and shadowy."

Mandy felt a shiver run down her spine. She didn't know whether to be frightened or fascinated by Ernie's spooky stories. They couldn't be true, could they? James glanced at her and she knew he felt the same.

"Well — I don't know what to make of all this," Grandma said. "It sounds very far-fetched."

Ernie gave another of his rusty laughs. "Even if it is, there's one good thing about it!"

"What's that?" asked Mandy a bit nervously.

"Sam Western's going to be hopping mad! With the field half-empty, he'll lose money. It serves him right. I never liked the idea of him benefiting from Wilfred Bennett's misfortunes!"

"I won't argue with that," said Grandpa.

"Hee-hee," Ernie chuckled. "There's nothing Sam Western can do about a ghost!"

"Well," Grandma said thoughtfully, "I'm not saying I believe a word of this. But there's no smoke without fire."

Five

Mandy and James paused by the town green, Ernie Bell's creepy stories still on their minds.

Suddenly, James waved his arms about and made loud "Woo-oo! Woo-oo!" noises. Then he rolled his eyes, gave a strangled groan, and sank onto the grass beneath the huge oak tree. Blackie capered around him, wagging his tail and licking his face.

"Don't!" Mandy fell down laughing. She couldn't think of a less frightening ghost — and Blackie was making enough noise to scare off a whole bunch of spooks!

"Do you think it's true about the ghostly horse and

rider?" James said, on his feet once again and brushing off the grass seeds sticking to his sweater.

"*Headless* rider!" Mandy said, still chuckling. "Yeah, right!"

"Didn't your grandma say Ernie's trying to fool you?" James asked with a grin.

Mandy felt her face get red, but she had to laugh. She knew she had a tendency to exaggerate. "Well, anyway, Grandpa says the whole story's probably just a bunch of nonsense."

James shrugged. "Do you agree with him?"

"I don't know. But there's one way to find out!"

"Do you mean go up there?" James looked alarmed.

"Yup. I'm okay with it if you are. What do you say?"

James put his head to one side. "Well — okay," he said uncertainly. "But it wouldn't do any good going in the daytime."

"No," agreed Mandy. "The ghostly horseman is only seen at night. We'd have to be up there pretty late." Suddenly, she saw problems looming. "What would we tell our parents?"

James scrunched up his face, thinking hard. Suddenly, he wagged his finger. "Hang on! I've got it — badgers!"

Mandy looked at him. "What have badgers got to do with this?"

"We could ask for permission to do a badger watch. The new family is up by the campsite, so it would almost be true."

"That's a great idea!"

"Here you go," Dr. Adam said that evening. "You can borrow these binoculars. They have special infrared night vision."

"Thanks, Dad." Mandy felt a little guilty as she promised to take good care of them.

"Hang on." Her dad was being very enthusiastic and helpful. "There won't be much of a moon. You'd better take this flashlight as well. It's dark in those woods."

"Okay." Mandy thrust the binoculars and flashlight into a backpack and slung it over her shoulder.

Dr. Adam began to sing, his rich voice filling the room. "Oh, Mandy went out one moonlit night."

Mandy ducked and hurried toward the door. Her dad could be so embarrassing sometimes.

"She prayed for the moon to give her light. For she had many a mile to go that night. Before she reached the town-o —" Her dad stopped abruptly and sang out, "Happy badger-watching!"

"Thanks!" she called out. "We'll make sure we're back just after ten."

It was just getting dark when she met James at the

crossroads. Bats were swooping low over the trees and the hollow hoot of an owl echoed across the fields. The moon had risen, looking like a nail paring.

James's eyes lit up behind his glasses after he looked through the binoculars. "Wow! Just what we need for ghost-busting!"

They pedaled hard to the edge of town but slowed down on the unlit winding bends. Soon Wilfred Bennett's house came into view. There was a light on in the kitchen window, but the rest of the house was dark. Mandy felt a pang at the thought of the old man in there all alone.

They stopped their bikes outside the campsite. The big, wooden fence looked black against a dark blue sky that was pricked by stars. Wind rustled through the trees, and from far off there came the strange, coughing bark of a fox. Suddenly it didn't seem like such a good idea to be up here by themselves. It was easy to imagine that a ghostly horseman would come sailing through the trees.

"What's the plan?" asked James, squaring his shoulders.

Mandy knew he was nervous but trying to hide it. "Let's put our bikes in the camping field. Then we can have a look around."

"Fine by me."

Mandy looked into the darkness as she wheeled her bike in through the gate and leaned it against a tree. She stood looking around. A faint light came from the old stable block, way off across the field. It was a dull beacon in a sea of darkness.

"There aren't many tents here," said James, his voice sounding shaky. "It's a little creepy, isn't it?"

Mandy usually thought that her nerves were as strong as steel. In the clinic she had seen her parents give blood transfusions, operate on stomachs, and stitch up wounds. But ghosts were another thing entirely.

"Maybe a little," she said, trying to put on a brave face.

Suddenly, James tensed. "What was that?"

Mandy jumped. "What?"

"I thought I heard something," James said. "Out on the road."

Mandy listened hard, but could hear nothing. "What kind of noise was it?"

"I don't know. Sort of like clopping. It's stopped now."

Mandy gulped. "The ghost!" She dug in her backpack for the flashlight as she ran for the gate.

"Wait for me!" James raced after her.

Suddenly, yapping like crazy, a small dog charged down the field and hurtled past them.

"Oh!" Mandy tripped and lost her grip on the flashlight. The dog had brushed past her legs, dashing toward the open gate. She recognized that brown-and-white shape. Sparky!

Recovering quickly, Mandy raced after the dog, reaching the gate just in time to see a car's headlights sweep the grass shoulder of the road in a wide arc. Still barking, Sparky leaped out into the road, straight into the path of the car.

"Look out!" Mandy screamed.

Too late. Car brakes screeched. There was a bang and a yelp of pain.

"Oh, no!"

Ghostly horsemen, strange noises, everything was forgotten as Mandy rushed toward a real-life emergency. The car had skidded across the road. As it came to a halt, the driver got out. He was a stocky, balding man in a dark suit. Shakily, he walked over to Mandy and James, who had gone straight to Sparky. He bent down and looked at the little dog as it lay on its side in the road.

"Oh, no. This is t-terrible," he stammered, looking up as Mandy threw herself to her knees beside the injured animal. "I swerved, but I couldn't miss it. Is it your dog?"

Mandy shook her head, gulping back tears, as she

reached out toward the little brown-and-white animal. "No. But I know him. His name's Sparky."

Although her hands shook, she felt herself grow calm. She had to help Sparky. The little dog's eyes opened briefly as she knelt beside him. Mandy spoke to him in a soothing, comforting voice. She knew that talking gently to hurt animals calmed them. It helped to keep their pulses steady if they were in shock.

Quickly she checked the dog's breathing. He was panting hard and there was a lot of blood on his back leg.

"Sparky! Oh, no!" Flora Pearson ran up to the small group huddled around her dog. She wrung her hands. Tears glistened on her cheeks. "The silly boy! He ran out of the tent before I could stop him. It was the sound of hoofbeats. He can't stand horses."

Without her red beret, Flora's hair stuck out in wispy strands. She wore a baggy orange T-shirt, with SAVE THE WHALES printed on it in large letters.

"Mandy knows what to do," James said. "Don't worry."

"Oh, yes. Mandy's the local vets' daughter, isn't she?" Flora said, rubbing at her eyes.

"It's going to be all right, Sparky," Mandy said softly.

The injured leg was bleeding badly. Somehow she had to try and stop the flow, but how? Then she remembered helping her mom treat a fox that had been caught in a trap. Quickly, she took a clean handkerchief out of her jeans pocket and tied it tightly around Sparky's leg in a makeshift bandage.

"There now, boy," she murmured as Sparky whimpered in pain.

The little dog turned his head. Mandy moved slowly and carefully; injured animals could snap. But Sparky only licked her hand feebly. He seemed grateful for her help.

"That'll help stop the bleeding," Mandy said. "But we have to take it off soon. The leg needs to be properly treated." She wished her mom or dad were there. Sparky needed expert care, and quickly.

The driver had been silent up to now. He still looked shaken. "Can I do anything?"

"Yes," Mandy said. "Can you drive us to Animal Ark, please? That's my parents' vet clinic."

"Sure." The man, who introduced himself as Bob Foster, took off his jacket. He spread it out. "You can use this as a stretcher."

Gently, with Flora's help, Mandy laid Sparky on top. Then everyone piled into the car.

Dr. Adam took one look at Mandy's flushed face and took charge. "Bring him straight through to the examining room," he said. "Mandy — I'll need your help. Would everyone else wait here, please?"

Mandy watched her dad scrub up and put on rubber gloves. "You did well, Mandy," he said over his shoulder. "That bandage certainly slowed the bleeding."

She held Sparky gently while her dad checked him over thoroughly, searching with his quick, practiced fingers.

"No internal injuries," Dr. Adam said after a while. "But that leg has a bad break. He could need an operation." He gave the little dog an injection and sedated him. "We'll need to do an X ray, but I suspect that bone will have to be pinned."

Mandy frowned with concern. "Will the leg heal properly?"

"It should," Dr. Adam said confidently. "Jack Russells are tough little things."

Mandy breathed a huge sigh of relief. She helped make Sparky comfortable in a large cage in the residential unit. When she left, the little dog had settled down with his nose between his paws.

"Have a good rest," she said as she left. "You've been very brave."

As Mandy and her dad came out into the waiting room, she heard Flora talking to Bob Foster. Bob was insisting on paying for Sparky's treatment.

"Whatever it costs," he said. "Poor little guy."

"Okay. If you insist. That's most kind." Flora's voice was firm, despite her being upset. She managed to look dignified in her baggy shorts and bright orange T-shirt. "But you really shouldn't blame yourself. Once he heard those hoofbeats, nothing could stop him."

Mandy was suddenly alert. That was the second time Flora had mentioned hoofbeats. And James had thought he heard a sound on the road, just before Sparky ran out. She was dying to ask Flora some questions, but now wasn't the time.

Catching sight of Dr. Adam, Flora paused; her thin face looked pale and strained. "How is he?"

Mandy's dad smiled. "Resting comfortably now. I'll need to check the X rays before I treat that leg. I'll do it first thing in the morning."

Flora lifted her chin. "Thank you," she said. She turned to Mandy. "And thank you. I don't know what I'd have done if . . ."

"That's okay," Mandy said quickly. She always got embarrassed when people thanked her.

Bob offered to give Flora a ride back to the campsite and drop James home on the way. "Oh," James said, remembering. "We left our bikes in the field."

"Oh, no! I left my backpack, too," Mandy said. "I must

have dropped it inside the gate." She looked up at her dad guiltily. His flashlight and binoculars were inside it. "Sorry, Dad."

"That's all right." Dr. Adam ruffled his daughter's hair. "You had other things on your mind."

Flora promised to look after the backpack and bikes, and Mandy and James arranged to go and get them the following day.

"It's a little late to go back up there now," Dr. Adam agreed, as he saw everyone to the door. When they had gone, he turned to Mandy. "One thing puzzles me."

"What's that, Dad?" Mandy said, walking toward the stairs, her blue eyes wide.

He lifted one dark eyebrow. "How many badgers were you expecting to see at the campsite?"

Saying something about a shortcut up to the woods, Mandy made a dash for the stairs. Over her shoulder, she saw that her dad was staring after her, a quizzical look on his face.

Just then, there was the sound of a car in the driveway. The front door opened and Emily Hope came in, looking tired. "Hi, everyone. I'm home!"

Adam Hope greeted his wife warmly. "How did it go?"

"It was a long day." Dr. Emily smiled. "The conference was fine. The dinner was, well, interesting!"

"We've had an interesting evening, too. Haven't we, Mandy?"

Mandy came downstairs to hug her mom briefly. "You tell Mom all about it, Dad. I'm bushed!" she said, pleading tiredness, and ran up to her bedroom.

Phew! she thought. *What a lucky escape!*

Six

Flora Pearson was sitting outside her tent when Mandy and James arrived early on Sunday morning. She was drinking coffee out of one of her bright tin mugs. Sparky's empty yellow mug sat on the grass to one side.

"How's Sparky?" asked Flora at once, pouring orange juice for Mandy and James.

"He's doing fine," Mandy said. "Dad didn't have to operate after all."

Flora nodded, the red beret bobbing. "But the leg was broken?"

Mandy nodded. "Dad said it was a clean break. He's set it and put a special plastic cast on it."

"Oh, no. Poor Sparky."

"It'll be all right," James said encouragingly. "Mandy's mom and dad are really good vets."

Flora's sudden grin enlivened her thin face. "Their daughter's pretty special, too!"

Mandy didn't think so. She had just done what needed doing. She was especially sensitive about road accidents because her own parents had been killed in a car crash. Adam and Emily Hope had adopted her when she was a baby, and now they were as real as any mom and dad could be.

"Dad says Sparky can come back up here tomorrow," Mandy said. "But he told me to tell you he wants to check to see if the leg is healing properly in a few days."

"Oh, that's fine. I'll make sure he gets lots of rest. I'll be staying at the site until he's completely recovered. No more hiking for a while!" She puffed out her bony chest, clad this morning in a lime-green T-shirt with the motto ANIMAL POWER embroidered across it. "It'll take more than a ghost to make me move on without my Sparky!"

"Dad said not to worry. He'll bring Sparky back up here in the Land Rover." Mandy suddenly realized what Flora had said. She gasped. "You saw the ghostly horseman?"

"Oh, yes," Flora said, as if it were the most normal thing

in the world. "Sparky and I were coming back from the Fox and Goose restaurant the night before last, when it appeared out of the mist." She chuckled. "I don't know who was more shocked, me or the phantom!"

"Wow!" James looked at Mandy, then back at Flora. "What did it look like?"

"Sort of pale and glowing — a horse and rider. I caught just a shadowy glimpse, then Sparky went into a frenzy, pulling at his leash and growling. I had a hard time trying to control him. By the time I looked up again — the ghost had gone."

"Weren't you scared?" Mandy asked.

Flora looked thoughtful for a moment, then she shook her head. "Not really. I know it sounds strange, but I had the feeling that it was more scared of me. It certainly ran off fast enough!"

Mandy and James sat in stunned silence as they finished their juice.

"And you think it came back last night?" Mandy asked at last.

"When you were inside your tent?" added James.

"Yes," Flora agreed. "This time, Sparky didn't wait to see it. As soon as he heard that clip-clopping outside the fence, he was up and out of the tent opening before I could grab him."

James gave a sudden shiver. "I think I might have heard it, too!" His voice sounded funny.

Mandy frowned. It was hard to believe in ghosts, but Flora had definitely seen something. A horse and rider, she had said. But there were no horses stabled around here anymore. Mandy didn't know what to think.

A short while later, Flora got Mandy's backpack from her tent. "Here you are, my dear. And your bikes are tied to the tree. I'll come and help you undo the knots."

Mandy and James watched in astonishment as Flora took hold of the complicated-looking knots and untied them with ease. "There. Nothing to it. I always could tie a terrific square knot!"

Flora decided to walk into Welford with them, as she wanted to visit Sparky. "I'll take him some of my home-made treats. That'll cheer him up."

Mandy grinned at James. They were both thinking the same thing. Good thing she wasn't going to take his yellow mug and make him a drink in the Animal Ark kitchen!

Outside the campsite, Mandy and James wheeled their bikes along beside Flora. Mandy glanced toward Wilfred's house as they passed by. Once again, there was no sign of their friend.

Flora swung her arms, striding along Welford Road.

They soon reached the town. At the top of the lane, Mandy and James paused.

"Animal Ark's just down there," Mandy said, pointing. "You can't miss it."

"Thanks. Everything looks so different in the daylight." Flora's face clouded as she remembered last night's harrowing journey in Bob Foster's car.

"Sparky was lucky," Mandy said.

"Yes." Flora's face brightened. She waved good-bye as Mandy and James got on their bikes. "See you soon!"

It was James's idea to go into the grocery store before the bike ride to school the following morning. He wanted to buy potato chips. Mandy was at the counter paying for her favorite treat, peppermint candy, when Ernie Bell came in.

"Hi, Mr. Bell," they chorused.

"Now then, you two," Ernie replied, a smile flickering across his grumpy face. He took a newspaper from the stand and nodded a greeting to Mrs. McFarlane, who was replacing the big glass jar of rainbow-striped peppermints on its shelf.

"Good morning, Ernie," Mrs. McFarlane said, ringing the cash register. Her round face lit up. "Have you heard the latest? The ghostly horseman was heard the night before last. A little dog ran after it and got knocked down by a car. The whole town's buzzing over it."

Mandy looked at Mrs. McFarlane in surprise. How had word spread so quickly?

"You two were up there, weren't you?" said the store owner. "Lucky for that poor dog. Did either of you see the ghost?"

Mandy shook her head and James did the same. It was best not to say anything. Her grandma said Mrs. McFarlane had a gift for making mountains out of molehills.

"Have you heard anything, Mr. Bell?" Mrs. McFarlane asked.

Ernie stroked his chin and suddenly became interested in the display of chocolate bars on the counter. James and Mandy exchanged glances. They knew Ernie loved good gossip just as much as Mrs. McFarlane, but sometimes he liked to pretend he was above such things.

"Anything at all?" the store owner encouraged.

"We-ell," Ernie began grudgingly. "I did hear that Sam Western's really mad about the whole thing." He gave one of his surprising rusty chuckles. "He was going on and on, apparently, saying that all this ghost nonsense is ruining his business."

Mrs. McFarlane's eyes crinkled. She crossed her arms in front of her and gave a long sigh. "It doesn't take much for that man to start complaining," she said with a disapproving sniff. "He thinks he can snap his fingers and make everyone do as he pleases."

"You're right," agreed Ernie. "Western's even got Dennis Saville looking into things for him."

"Hmmph!" snorted Mrs. McFarlane. "That man needs a change of attitude."

Mandy and James looked at each other, trying not to laugh. For once they agreed with her.

"Saville won't have much luck," commented Ernie, his head to one side. "You can't stop people from talking, no matter how much you try."

Ernie paid for his newspaper and bought a bag of peanuts for Sammy, his pet squirrel. He pocketed his change and turned to go. At the door he waved to Mandy and James.

"I'm on my way to Lilac Cottage to finish that fence panel. Young Tom's got no idea about carpentry. No idea at all."

The bell rang as the door closed, and Mandy and James burst out laughing.

"What?" Mrs. McFarlane said, her nose in the air like a bloodhound on a fresh trail. "Is it a private joke, or can anyone join in?"

Still chuckling, Mandy and James ran for the door.

*   *   *

"Well — what do you think?" Grandpa said, his arms spread wide in front of the new fence panel. "Countersunk screws and everything!"

"A perfect job!" Mandy said with a grin. It was a beautiful clear evening; she and James had come to Lilac Cottage for a snack, after a busy day at school.

"You have to hand it to Ernie," her grandma said. "He's difficult and pigheaded, but he knows his stuff."

"He does," Grandpa said. "He huffed and puffed a little, but I caught him smiling when he thought I wasn't looking. He really enjoyed showing me the ropes!"

They all chuckled.

"I hear you two have been busy, too," Grandma said. "How's that little dog?"

Mandy told her that Sparky was doing well. "He managed to limp a few steps this morning. Dad's surprised how well he's doing."

"The accident must have happened almost outside Wilfred Bennett's house," Grandma said thoughtfully.

"Yes, it did," said James. "Just yards away."

"You didn't happen to see any sign of Wilfred, did you?" asked Grandma, glancing meaningfully at her husband.

"No." Mandy saw the look. "We've been up near his house a couple of times, but we haven't seen him. Why?"

"Your grandma's getting a little worried about the guy," Grandpa said.

"It's just that no one in town has seen Wilfred for ages," Grandma said. "I was going up to visit him this morning, but I didn't have time to, and Mrs. Ponsonby's coming over in half an hour. There's something she wants me to bring to the committee." Grandma was chairwoman of the Welford Women's Club.

"Hmmph!" Grandpa gave Mandy a look. "That's most of the evening taken up, then. That woman never uses one word when ten would do!"

Mandy chuckled. "We could go and visit Wilfred. Couldn't we, James?"

He nodded.

"Would you, sweetheart?" Grandma said. "It would put my mind at ease."

If only my mind was at ease, Mandy thought. She wanted to make sure Wilfred was okay, but she also wanted to ask him about Matty. This time, she was determined to find out where the little old mare had gone. It was only a few days since the horse auction, but it felt like weeks since she had last set eyes on Matty.

"Why don't you pick some vegetables, Dorothy?" Grandpa said to his wife. "Mandy and James can take some to Wilfred."

"Good idea," Grandma said. "That lettuce needs picking before it rots."

"I'll leave it to you," Grandpa said. "I'm just going to

put a coat of polyurethane on this panel." He winked at Mandy. "Unless I'm needed."

Grandma gave him a playful push. "Go ahead! I think we can manage."

Mandy, James, and Grandma picked their way past rows of young peas and beans. They pulled up lettuce, dug up young carrots and beets, and gathered bunches of spring onions.

"Here. You can pile them in this old basket," Grandma said, shaking loose soil from the roots. "There. Don't they look good?"

Mandy nodded. The basket, framed with carrot tops and red-veined beet leaves, looked as colorful as could be. "Wilfred's going to love these."

A few minutes later, there was a knock on the front door. Grandma went to open it. With a sinking heart, Mandy heard her say, "Oh, hello, Amelia. You're early."

"I prefer to be prompt," said a rich, bossy voice. "Punctuality is my middle name."

"I thought it was Bossy!" joked James.

Mrs. Ponsonby sailed into the house, resplendent in a powder-blue dress and a matching flowery hat. Pandora was, as usual, under her arm, a matching ribbon holding the fur out of her eyes. Toby, her other dog, was trotting by her side.

"Uh-oh." *Time to make an exit*, thought Mandy. She

signaled to James and he nodded eagerly. Stooping to give Toby a hasty pat, they made their way out the front door, saying their good-byes as they went.

"My goodness! Young people today. Always in such a hurry." Mrs. Ponsonby's voice faded as Mandy paused in the driveway to loop the basket over her handlebars.

They pedaled through the town and on toward Wilfred's house. On the outskirts, they crested the final hill and the house came into view.

"This is getting to be a habit!" James said with a grin, propping his bike against the new fence.

"Maybe we should bring our tents next time!" Mandy replied.

Wilfred's house had that same deserted look to it. Mandy rapped the horse-shaped knocker. There was some movement near the kitchen curtains, then a hurried scuffling sound from inside the house.

"What can he be doing in there?" said James.

"I don't know," Mandy answered.

After a long pause, they heard the sound of bolts being unlatched. Wilfred opened the door a crack, giving them only a glimpse of the shadowy interior.

"Now then," he said, his usual friendly greeting, but his voice sounded thin and wary. His flyaway white hair looked as if it hadn't been combed in days.

"Hi, Wilfred," Mandy said with a warm smile. "We've brought you some vegetables from Grandma's garden."

She thought the old man looked very tired and drawn, but he returned her smile. "That's very kind of you two." He reached for the basket. "Tell your grandma thanks. It's much appreciated."

Mandy held on to the basket. "We haven't seen you in town lately," she said.

"No. I haven't really done much," Wilfred said vaguely. "I keep myself to myself. It's best that way."

"I'd love to go and visit Matty," Mandy began, trying a new approach. "If you would just tell me where . . ."

"Um, I have to go now, kids," Wilfred said, looking flustered.

He began to close the door but got the basket caught in the doorway. As he opened the door to free it, the frayed cuff of his cardigan snagged on a loose piece of wicker.

"Oh, no!" Wilfred muttered in dismay, as the basket tipped forward. The front door swung open. Spring onions flew everywhere, carrots bounced off the step, and beets rolled into the house.

"Oh!" James hurried forward, bending to gather up an escaping lettuce.

While Wilfred was still trying to untangle himself

from the basket, Mandy stepped inside the doorway to chase carrots and beets down the hall.

"Oh, dear me," Wilfred said in a panicky voice, following as Mandy and James walked farther into the house, their hands full. "It's all right. I can manage now. Really, there's no need for you to come in."

But Mandy was already inside the big old-fashioned kitchen. She dropped the vegetables in the deep sink, her mind registering that things looked very much cluttered and untidy.

"Sorry about the mess," Wilfred said uneasily, looking embarrassed. "I spend all my time in here now," he said, a fleeting sadness passing over his face. "I don't need much space. And I feel closest to Rose in here."

Mandy nodded, feeling sad and a little puzzled. It wasn't like the Wilfred she knew to live in such chaos. But as she looked around, Mandy realized that it wasn't just an ordinary mess that cluttered the kitchen. The oak dresser was piled with things that had come from the living room at the back of the house. She remembered dusting those vases in the living room when she had come to the house with Grandma, to help out when Rose had been ill.

On one shelf, there was Rose's collection of china horses and the little foal Mandy had bought for Rose's last birthday.

There also was the special photo, the one of Rose standing with a much younger Matty. Sunlight highlighted the silver in the mare's coat. Rose's hair was dark and her face was creased in a bright smile. A handwritten inscription in the corner read, "My Matty."

It seemed as though Wilfred had moved these things from the living room out of harm's way. *But why?* Mandy wondered. It was very strange.

"Well — thanks again," Wilfred said, looking more agitated and worried. "It was nice to see you." He began trying to usher them to the door, the sleeves of his tattered old cardigan trailing over his thin hands.

Then Mandy noticed the rolled-up rug leaning in one corner. It was the one that usually covered the living room floor. What was going on?

"Wilfred —" she began. Then she broke off in amazement as a most unexpected — but familiar — sound rang out. The sound of a horse neighing.

But not just any horse . . .

James looked at her, his mouth hanging open.

For a moment, Mandy was too stunned to utter a word. Could it really be . . . "Matty?" she gasped.

Wilfred's shoulders sagged. He looked at her and gave a deep sigh. "Yes," he said gently. "You've found me out."

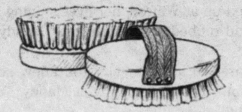

Seven

"You'd better come in," Wilfred said, leading the way.

Mandy's heart was beating fast as she and James followed him. She couldn't believe it. Wilfred had been keeping Matty in the house!

The curtains were drawn in the living room and in the semidarkness Matty's pale coat glowed. Something clicked in the back of Mandy's mind, but she was too delighted to see Matty again to pay attention to it. The elderly little horse turned her head and whinnied softly in greeting.

"Oh, Matty." Mandy rushed forward and threw her arms around the mare's neck. "It's so good to see you!"

She looked up at Wilfred, her eyes shining as Matty whinnied and rubbed her head against Mandy's shoulder.

James stared in amazement. "You knew something was going on," he said, glancing at Mandy. "You were right all along!"

"Yes, but I never expected this!" Mandy hugged Matty's neck delightedly and buried her face in the pale mane.

Wilfred looked at Matty, his lined old face wistful. "When it came to the morning of the horse sale, I just couldn't bear to part with her. Not with her being Rose's favorite and all. But I just didn't know what to do. I had nowhere to put her."

Thinking of the photo of Rose with Matty, Mandy felt a lump rise in her throat. She swallowed hard and looked around. Wilfred shouldn't be keeping Matty in here, but he had done his best. The furniture had been pushed against the wall and covered with sheets. Straw had been spread on the stone floor. A bucket of water stood in the corner and a hay net hung from a hook on the door.

Mandy stroked Matty's velvety nose, noticing that the little mare's eyes were bright and her coat soft and glossy. She certainly seemed happy enough, but for how much longer?

"You're not planning to go on keeping her in the house, are you?" she asked Wilfred worriedly.

Wilfred ran his fingers through his straggly white hair. "No. It was only supposed to be for a couple of days. Just until I figured something out. I've made countless phone calls, trying to find someone I know and trust who'll take Matty. But it's been a week now, and I've almost run out of people to try."

He sank down wearily onto the arm of a sofa. "To tell you the truth," he said, shoulders drooping, "I've been at my wits' end with all this. I don't know if I'm coming or going."

Mandy remembered the cluttered kitchen. Poor Wilfred. She thought Matty looked in better shape than he did. It all seemed too much for the man.

"It must have been hard to keep this a secret," said James.

"Yes, it was." Wilfred looked up. "I was worried at first that someone would hear Matty, but all that commotion going on next door hid any noise she made. It's been harder to keep things secret since the campsite opened. But Matty doesn't need much exercise. She's been content with going out at night, when there's no one around. But I know this can't go on much longer — it's not fair for either of us."

Mandy and James shook their heads sympathetically.

Then Mandy gasped. "Oh!" She looked at James. Suddenly, everything fell into place. The silver-gray horse and her rider — a man with white hair.

"The ghostly horseman!" said James, guessing her thoughts.

Wilfred looked puzzled. "What's that?"

"Some of the campers have seen you riding Matty at night," Mandy explained. "But they knew there were no horses stabled near here anymore."

James continued the story, "So, they thought it was a ghostly horse and rider! In the mist and moonlight you must have looked really spooky. People are saying the campsite's haunted! Sam Western's furious about the whole thing."

Wilfred shook his head from side to side. "Oh, dear! I had no idea that all this was going on. I seem to have caused a lot of trouble."

"You didn't mean to," Mandy said.

"No, I didn't," agreed Wilfred. "But Sam Western won't see it like that. Once he hears about this there will be fireworks."

"He won't hear anything from me," muttered James.

"Or me," Mandy found herself echoing. It might not be right to keep Matty in the house, but she knew that Wilfred's intentions had been well-meaning.

"You mean — you'll keep my secret?" Wilfred looked surprised, but pleased.

"Yes. But on one condition," Mandy said. She saw James looking at her curiously.

"What's that?" Wilfred said.

"That until Matty goes to her new home, James and I can help you look after her!" James smiled and nodded in agreement.

"We-ell." Wilfred considered their offer, then his face broadened in a smile. "All right. I must admit, I'd be glad to have an extra hand or two."

"Great!" said James with a perfectly straight face. "Then you'll be even happier to have four!"

They all laughed.

"I don't like the idea of you two covering up for me," Wilfred said.

"It's not exactly covering up," Mandy said. "Not if we just don't talk about you and Matty to anyone in town."

"That's right," James agreed.

"And Mom and Dad won't tell anyone," Mandy began eagerly, "once we explain. They might be able to help." She paused, noticing that Wilfred was looking a bit sheepish.

"I'd rather you didn't tell your parents, either. Not just yet," he said. "I've got one last person to see about Matty. I'd really like to find her a home myself. I've got my pride, you know? I know I got into a mess with the business and everything, but if I can just see that Matty's settled, well — it'll make things right. I owe that to Rose."

"But what if this person can't take Matty, either?" Mandy asked worriedly.

Wilfred lifted his head, a determined look on his face. "Matty's well-being has to come first," he said stoutly. "If this last lead comes to nothing in the next few days, I'll be only too glad to ask for Adam's help."

Mandy nodded. "Okay." She knew her softhearted dad would understand if she kept Wilfred's secret. It was in a good cause. Mom might be another story. But she'd worry about that when she came to it.

James nodded in agreement.

"Well," Wilfred said with a grin, "with any luck, it'll only be for another day or two. Once Matty's settled into her new home, I couldn't care less if the whole story comes out and if Sam Western complains until he's blue in the face!"

Mandy chuckled. Wilfred was beginning to sound more like his jaunty old self. She put out a hand and rubbed Matty's nose. "Can James and I start helping you with Matty now?"

She was itching to start taking care of the little horse.

It seemed so long since she had groomed that beautiful, silver-gray coat and braided the flowing mane and tail.

"I don't see why not," Wilfred said, smiling. He reached up and moved the curtains open a little bit, so that a shaft of sunlight, swirling with dust motes, poured into the room. By the extra light, Mandy saw again how tired and gaunt he looked. James had noticed, too.

"I think we can manage in here by ourselves," Mandy said casually.

"Easy as pie!" James said, following her lead.

Wilfred stood up tall. He seemed about to protest, but then he changed his mind. "To tell you the truth, I'm dying for a cup of coffee," he said. "Go ahead. I'll just show you where everything is."

"Great," said Mandy, pushing up her sleeves.

Wilfred took them out to the tiny backyard. There was an old storage bin beside the back door. Wilfred opened it. Inside, there was a plastic bin with oats and bran and two small piles of hay and straw.

"Got everything you need? Then I'll leave you to it." Wilfred went back into the kitchen.

"Oh, look," Mandy said. "He's kept all Matty's grooming equipment." She took out the plastic tray with all its different brushes, currycombs, and sponges. There was even a straw wisp for massaging that Wilfred had made himself. Everything was well used but spotlessly clean.

"He really does love that horse," James said.

Mandy sighed. "If only there was some way he could keep her." *But where?* she thought. *You can't keep a horse for long without stables and land.*

Back in the living room, Mandy and James got to it. It was hard work. First, Mandy raked out the old straw and dumped it into the tiny yard. There was no room for a muck heap, so James forked it into the black plastic garbage bags Wilfred had given them.

"No wonder Wilfred looks so tired," said James.

Mandy nodded, imagining Wilfred having to stay up late every night to exercise Matty.

Mandy swept the stone floor while James got fresh bedding. "There's not much straw left," he said as he helped Mandy spread the new straw evenly with a rake. "We'll have to remember to tell Wilfred."

While James went out and refilled the water bucket, Mandy dealt with the hay net. As soon as she'd hung it back on its hook, Matty stretched her neck and began pulling out wisps of fresh hay with her angled, yellow teeth.

"It's so nice to see her again, isn't it?" Mandy said,

running a hand down the mare's sleek side. Matty's ears swiveled as if she knew what Mandy was saying. "I wish I'd gotten a treat for her."

"You should have brought some of your dad's carrot sticks!" joked James.

Mandy laughed. "I know just what Dad would say — 'She's welcome to them!'"

"Hang on a sec. Why don't we give her a couple of those carrots your grandma sent for Wilfred?"

"Good idea," Mandy said. "I'm sure Wilfred won't mind."

They found him in the kitchen. Wilfred had been busy, too. Clean dishes were piled on the drain board and freshly scrubbed pots and pans hung from their hooks.

"Now then," he said, looking more relaxed than they had seen him for weeks. "How are you two doing?"

"We've finished the cleaning up," Mandy said.

"Already? My, you're hard workers!"

"We don't waste any time!" James said with a grin.

"Can we have a couple of Grandma's carrots for Matty?" asked Mandy.

"You go right ahead," Wilfred said.

Mandy rinsed off the soil, then chopped the carrots into lengthways strips; she knew that square or round pieces could get stuck in a horse's throat. Wilfred came in and watched as she fed the sweet young carrots to Matty.

He looked down at the clean, fresh straw. "You've done a great job," he said.

Mandy smiled. That made all their hard work worthwhile. The little horse finished crunching up the carrots. Whinnying softly, she nudged against Mandy's jeans pocket.

"I'm sorry I didn't bring you a red apple," Mandy said with a happy grin. "But I'll bring you one next time. That's a promise!"

She gave Matty a final pat. She hated leaving the little mare so soon after finding her again, but it wouldn't be for long.

Wilfred came to the front door to wave good-bye. "Thanks a lot, you two."

"That's okay, Wilfred."

Wilfred coughed a little. "Matty really appreciated the visit, you know," he said, his voice sounding gruff. "The two of us get along okay together, but Matty misses Rose. She's used to a woman's company."

"We'll come again before school tomorrow," Mandy began. "Oh, I almost forgot. You'll need some more straw soon."

"Oh, no," Wilfred murmured, beginning to look worried again. "I knew I was getting low. It's going to arouse suspicion in town if I'm seen buying straw."

"Don't worry. You leave that to us," Mandy said firmly.

She had no idea how she and James were going to get some straw for Matty, but she was sure they would think of something.

Eight

Mandy soon found out that it was more difficult to keep Wilfred's secret than she'd imagined.

"Your grandma said you took some fresh vegetables up to Wilfred the other evening," Dr. Emily said.

Mandy had changed out of her school uniform. She and her mom were eating dinner alone before early evening office hours started. Her dad was still out doing routine inoculations at some of the isolated farms.

"Mmm," Mandy said, taking a huge bite of crusty French bread. She chewed slowly, hoping her mom wouldn't ask any more questions.

"Did you see Wilfred?" Dr. Emily prompted.

Mandy nodded, making "uh-huh" sounds.

"And how was he?"

Mandy tried to look casual. "Fine," she mimed with her mouth still full.

Dr. Emily stood up and put a white lab coat on over her clothes. She frowned, looking closely at her daughter with suspicious green eyes, but she only said, "Well, I'm glad to hear he's okay."

"Phew!" Mandy sighed. It had sounded so simple when she had promised Wilfred that she wouldn't talk about him or Matty!

She and James had been going up to help Wilfred with Matty after school for the past couple of days. Not only was it becoming more difficult to keep Wilfred's secret, the need for straw had become serious.

Mandy bumped into Simon as she was slipping inside the Animal Ark store room. Inside there were cans and packets of every kind of animal food and enough straw for an elephant. She had been hoping that she could smuggle out some straw for Matty.

"Hi there," said Simon. "What are you up to?" His short blond hair stuck up in spikes where he had dragged his fingers through it.

"Um, some straw," Mandy blurted out guiltily.

"Do you need some for Flopsy, Mopsy, and Cottontail?" Simon said helpfully.

Mandy's three pet rabbits were in their run, and their hutch was cleaned out and pristine, but she nodded, watching as he grabbed handfuls of straw and stuffed it into a plastic shopping bag.

"There you go. I'll put it outside the back door for you." Simon's eyes were friendly behind his glasses.

"Thanks," Mandy said. There was only enough straw there to cover a foot of Wilfred's stone floor, but it was a start.

"Are you in a rush?" asked Simon. "Your mom's got someone coming into the examination room with a pet you might like to see."

Mandy followed him eagerly. She could always find time to see a new patient.

"Oh." Mandy's eyes widened when she saw the tortoise. Its shell was a shiny dome as big as a beach ball. The head and legs were drawn in closely beneath the shell.

"He's handsome, isn't he?" said the owner. Mrs. Bland was a well-dressed woman who owned a moving business in Walton. "I've had Thomas almost thirty years."

"He's nice looking," Mandy agreed. "What's wrong with him, Mom?"

"He's been losing weight," Emily Hope said, turning to Mrs. Bland. "What do you feed him?"

"All kinds of things, like lettuce and dandelion leaves.

He loves strawberries, but he hasn't even been eating them lately." She looked worried. "Is it something serious?"

Dr. Emily asked Simon to help while she examined the heavy tortoise. Simon held Thomas's shell, careful to avoid the scaly feet that scratched against the examination table. Thomas's claws were strong and curved and capable of inflicting a nasty gash.

"See if you can coax him to put his head out," Dr. Emily said to Mandy.

Mandy spoke to the tortoise gently and stroked one of his forelegs reassuringly. After a few minutes, Thomas stuck out his long, wrinkled neck. He blinked slowly, then yawned.

"Ah, I see the problem," her mom said at once. "Can you see it, Mandy?"

"His beak looks a little strange," Mandy said.

"That's right. It's overgrown." Dr. Emily turned to Thomas's owner. "That's why he's having a problem eating. I'll just trim his beak and he'll be fine."

"Oh, dear," Mrs. Bland said. "It won't hurt him, will it?"

"No," said Dr. Emily. She selected a pair of stainless-steel clippers from the sterilizing tray. "It's just like cutting your fingernails."

Mandy helped Simon hold Thomas still. A couple of

snips, carefully angled so that Thomas's beak kept the same shape, and it was done.

"Oh, that's a relief!" Mrs. Bland said. "Thank you so much." She picked Thomas up and went out of the exam room.

"Thanks for your help, Mandy," Simon said. "Are you going now? Don't forget that bag of —"

"Um, right," Mandy said quickly, catching her mom's eye. "Got to go! Bye, Simon. Bye, Mom! I'll be back in a couple of hours."

She hurried out into the reception area before her mom could ask any awkward questions. Jean Knox was behind the desk, her head bent over the appointment book as she flipped through its pages.

"Oh, hello, Mandy." Jean looked up and gave a flustered smile. "Did you want your mom? She's in the exam room."

"Hi, Jean! It's all right. I've just seen her."

"Okay, then, dear," Jean said, still searching for something. "Now where have I put those . . ."

"They're on the chain around your neck," Mandy said, trying not to giggle. Jean was always losing her glasses!

"Thanks, dear!" Jean called out as Mandy headed for the door into the house. "Silly me. It's a good thing my head's not loose!"

Mandy took three red apples from the bowl of fruit

on the kitchen table. Pausing only to get the plastic bag of straw, she hurried out to the road.

James was waiting at the town green, his bike leaning against the neatly clipped hedge. He looked bored. He had a piece of grass held between his thumbs and was blowing on it, making sounds like a quacking duck.

"Sorry I'm late." As Mandy lifted the shopping bag off her handlebars, James looked at it, a dubious expression on his face. "I know!" she said with a rueful smile. "It wouldn't even last a hamster five minutes!"

"You said it!" James grinned. "Couldn't you get any more?"

Mandy shook her head. "No. Simon would have been suspicious."

"Simon?" James said. "What's he got to do with it?"

He got no answer. Mandy suddenly had a brainstorm. "I know where there's *loads* of straw!" she said, turning her bike around. "Come on."

"Where to?" asked James.

"Grandpa's shed! He and Grandma are away on one of their trips today, but he keeps the key in the mailbox."

A few minutes later, they had arrived at Lilac Cottage. They stood looking at the bale of straw that Grandpa planned to spread over his strawberry beds.

"Perfect!" Mandy exclaimed.

"Oh, no! We can't," James said, suddenly concerned.

"It's the only way," Mandy said decisively. "Matty needs bedding. Where else are we going to get this much straw?"

"But won't your grandpa notice it's been stolen?"

"Borrowed," Mandy said firmly. "He said he wasn't planning to use it for a day or two. We'll have thought of a way to replace it by then."

"Will we?" James took a deep breath. "Okay. What if we do 'borrow' it? How are we going to get it up to Wilfred?"

Mandy bit her lip in concentration. "It's not that heavy. I know! We'll prop it on our bikes and wheel it up there."

"We could," James said, still looking doubtful. "But someone in town is bound to see us. You can't exactly disguise a bale of straw!"

Mandy grinned. If you were determined enough, there was always a way. "You can if you cover it with something."

"Like what?"

"This!" She reached up and took down an old rug that Grandpa put over his cold frame in cold weather.

James eyed the rug's yellow zigzag pattern. "It's a little bright."

"It's all we have. It'll just have to do."

"Okay," said James. "Let's do it. I'll get the bikes."

After a bit of a struggle, they managed to get the bale positioned so that it was balanced between the bikes. Mandy covered it with the rug, tying it down with some of Grandpa's garden twine. She gripped her handlebars, while James grabbed hold of his on the opposite side. "Ready? Let's go."

At first, it was pretty funny. James made her laugh, thinking of the silly things they could say if anyone asked them what they were doing. "How about — we're having an evening picnic and we're very, very hungry!" he suggested. Then they reached the first hill and they had no energy for talking, let alone laughing.

Almost an hour later, tired, red-faced, and dying for a cold drink, they stumbled up to Wilfred's front door. This time, Wilfred was expecting them. He opened the door almost at once.

"Wow! What's that contraption you've got there?" he said, his white eyebrows shooting up in amazement.

"It's straw under here," Mandy could only gasp.

"For Matty," James managed to get out.

"Bring it round back, then," Wilfred said, catching on fast. "Did anybody see you bringing it up here?"

"No," Mandy explained once she'd caught her breath.

"It was amazing. We didn't meet a single person." There had been a tough moment, when they had to go past the front of the grocery store. But Mrs. McFarlane had not noticed them.

"It's perfect. It's just what I need," Wilfred said. He helped lift the bale off the bikes and stowed it in the old storage container, then he took his wallet out of his pants pocket. "How much do I owe you?"

"We-ell," Mandy began, looking a bit sheepish. "It's hard to say."

"Huh? What do you mean?"

"It's not exactly ours. We borrowed it from my grandpa's shed."

"You did?" Wilfred began to chuckle. "And you wheeled it through town! Tom Hope will skin me alive if he thinks I put you up to this!"

"No, he won't. We'll explain," Mandy said. "Besides, he might not notice it's gone."

"And pigs might fly," muttered James. He had a sudden thought. "What did you do with that little plastic bag of straw that Simon gave you?"

"Uh-oh." Mandy's hand flew to her mouth. "I left it in Grandpa's shed!"

"That will surprise him!" Wilfred was laughing so much that his shoulders were shaking. "I'd like to be a fly on the wall when Tom finds out that his bale of straw has magically turned into a few handfuls in a plastic bag!"

Mandy and James began laughing, too. It was hard not to see the funny side, and Wilfred's laugh was infectious.

Wilfred wiped his eyes on the back of his hand. "My, you kids make me laugh. Come inside and have a cold drink."

Mandy and James collapsed on kitchen chairs while Wilfred looked in the fridge. "Oh. I've only got orange juice, I'm afraid. I'm sorry there's no lemonade or Coke."

"Juice is fine, thanks," Mandy said. She drained her glass in one gulp, then jumped up and put her used glass in the sink. "Can we go and see Matty now?"

"I thought you'd never ask," Wilfred said. "Go on in."

As they entered, Matty turned her head and whinnied softly.

"Hello, old girl," Mandy said, putting her arms around Matty's neck. She laid her cheek against the mare's satiny shoulder.

Matty breathed softly on Mandy's cheek. Then she dipped her neck and nudged Mandy's arm.

"Yes, I remembered your apples!" Mandy laughed. "Red ones. Your favorite."

Matty's soft lips nuzzled her palm as she took the first apple. Mandy stroked Matty's dark gray nose as the mare crunched up the fruit and chewed contentedly.

Mandy was longing to slip a bridle onto her and lead her out into the fresh air.

Just then, Wilfred came into the backroom. "I've just been on the phone with that friend I told you about," he said to Mandy and James. "The one who I thought might take Matty."

"Is he going to take her?" Mandy asked eagerly.

Wilfred stroked his chin, looking weary. "He says he's not sure. He thinks she's too old." He shook his head, looking desperate. "I was banking on him taking her. I don't know who else to ask."

"What about the horse auctions?" suggested James in his practical way. "Couldn't you sell Matty there? Like you sold your other horses?"

Wilfred looked at him and shook his head slowly. "I can't face her going to strangers — not if there's the slightest chance of an alternative. I've been trying to think if there's someone I haven't tried. There *must* be somebody I know who'd want her."

But time was running out. Mandy felt it and she knew Wilfred did, too. He had to find a solution and very soon, for Matty's sake.

Wilfred stroked Matty's neck. "She needs a field where she can run free," he said sadly. "I'm trying my best, but I'm afraid it'll have to be moonlight rides for just a little longer."

"We can come up and help you exercise her, can't we, James?" Mandy said.

James nodded.

The old man brightened. "You'd be doing me a favor. But are you sure you'll be allowed up here so late at night?"

"Oh, yes," Mandy said. "Well, for the next couple of days, anyway. It's Friday tomorrow, so we get to stay up later — no school the following day."

James grinned. "I can feel another badger watch coming on!"

The next day, Mandy could hardly concentrate on her lessons. Rather than go straight over to help Wilfred after school, she and James planned to go over later, in order to be around for Matty's exercise time.

As soon as she had helped clean up after dinner, Mandy excused herself. On the way to her room she picked out three apples from the fruit bowl.

A little while later, she popped her head into the living room door and waved to her dad. Dr. Adam was sprawled in front of the TV, tired out after a long day. He waved back, a half-eaten apple in his hand.

"Have you got everything for the badger watch?" her mom asked.

"Yup." Mandy patted her backpack. "Flashlight and

binoculars," she said. *Riding hat. And three more apples for Matty*, she added to herself.

"Okay, then. Have a good time, but be careful. See you just after ten — no later!" Dr. Emily went into the living room.

Mandy flew down the hall and almost tripped over a loose shoelace. She paused in the open front doorway to tie it and heard her dad say, "Was that Mandy I just saw flitting through? Or was it a mirage?"

"I wish I had half her energy," Dr. Emily said with a chuckle. There was a pause, then she said, "I think I'll have an apple as well."

"Oh, sorry. This was the last one left," her dad said. "It's funny. The fruit bowl was almost full this morning."

Mandy was up like a flash and out the front door before her dad had finished the sentence.

"Oh, no," said James when she told him about the apples. "You don't think your mom and dad have caught on to us, do you?"

"Not yet," Mandy said. "But if Grandpa calls about his straw, they're bound to put two and two together."

"And figure out exactly what's been going on these past few days," groaned James.

They reached Wilfred's house and stopped outside on

the road. Just a few yards away was the sign that read, WESTERN'S CAMPSITE. And past that, the gate stood wide open.

Mandy remembered the scene in the campsite from the night of Sparky's accident. The few lights glowing in the darkness had seemed only to emphasize the field's emptiness. She imagined Flora's low tent, all lit up from inside, looking cozy and welcoming.

"I bet Sparky's being spoiled rotten," James said. "Treats in bed and everything!"

Mandy grinned. "Flora brought him into Animal Ark for his checkup yesterday evening. Dad says his leg's healing really well."

"Good," James said. "It's Saturday tomorrow, so we'll have time to go and visit him." He followed Mandy around to the back of Wilfred's house. "At least we don't have to worry about him chasing after the ghostly horse tonight."

"No," Mandy agreed. "Flora's determined that he rest that leg. She's probably got his leash looped to the tent post!"

Wilfred was waiting for them with Matty in the living room. While they changed Matty's straw and water, Wilfred put her in a bridle. "It's safer for walking her near the road," he said.

He brought the reins over Matty's head and offered them to Mandy. "Do you want to take her? James and I will follow you."

"Oh, yes," Mandy breathed. She quickly put on her riding hat, then took the reins. She was a bit nervous as she led Matty out the back door.

The tiny yard was cramped, so it was difficult to turn the little horse and bring her down the side of the house, but Matty behaved beautifully, bending her neck so that Mandy didn't need to pull her around. "Good girl," Mandy said, patting her neck.

"That was neatly done, Mandy," Wilfred said.

Mandy smiled. "Rose showed me how to do that."

They walked down the side of the new fence to a narrow strip of field at the roadside. Wilfred explained that they must warm Matty up slowly. "Because she spends the day just standing in the house, there's the risk of a strained muscle if she's ridden too much without a careful warm-up."

Mandy and James took turns riding Matty, walking and trotting the elderly mare while Wilfred supervised. Mandy sat firmly in the saddle, enjoying every moment. It was wonderful to be riding the little mare again.

"Once you've had your rides, I'll take Matty out on the road," Wilfred said. "She enjoys a good long gallop."

Matty seemed to be enjoying the exercise. She moved

easily and fluidly, the muscles working under her pale coat. Mandy was watching as James trotted by on Matty, when she noticed a slight reluctance in the horse's movements. Matty seemed to be hanging back and pulling a little on the reins.

Mandy pointed it out to Wilfred. "I think Matty's had enough exercise for now," she said.

Wilfred frowned. "We haven't been out here all that long." He ran his hands down Matty's side and checked her legs. "She's not weak or anything," he said. "But I think we'll take her back inside."

Back in the house, Wilfred hung up the tackle, then began wiping Matty down with a handful of straw. Mandy helped dry off the mare's coat, then give her a brisk brush-down. The mare's head was drooping a little and she was shifting her weight from foot to foot. Now and then she pawed at the ground.

"I think I'll make her up a warm bran mash," Wilfred said thoughtfully. He turned to Mandy and James. "It's late. I think you two should be getting home."

"Okay," Mandy said. "We'll come back again in the morning."

"We can stay longer tomorrow," James added, "because it's Saturday."

"Yes," Wilfred said. "And thanks again. You've been a great help."

Mandy and James gave Matty a final pat. "See you tomorrow."

At the door, Mandy glanced back at Matty. The mare raised her head and whinnied softly.

Mandy was quiet as she and James biked home. "What's wrong?" asked James as they stopped outside his house.

"It's Matty. I think something's wrong with her."

"She seemed all right when we left," said James.

"I know, but I've got a funny feeling."

"Uh-oh." James looked at her. "What are you going to do?"

Mandy shrugged, miserable. "I don't know. I wish I could talk to Mom or Dad."

"You can't!" James replied. "We promised Wilfred."

"I know," Mandy said. "But if Matty's sick I've got to do something! Wilfred needs help."

The problem occupied her thoughts as she biked the short distance to Animal Ark. It was still on her mind as she got ready for bed. She lay awake for ages, staring into the dark and worrying about Wilfred and Matty.

Nine

Early the next morning, Mandy jumped out of bed and threw on some jeans and a sweater. She had to know if Matty was all right. She dashed downstairs, all set to excuse herself from breakfast and her morning chores in Animal Ark. Her dad was on the telephone in the hall and the look on his face stopped her in her tracks.

"Sounds like it could be colic," he said. "What's she doing now? Okay. I'll get over there right away."

Mandy's heart plummeted. "That was Wilfred, wasn't it? Oh, I knew Matty didn't look well! Can I come with you?"

Dr. Adam looked at his daughter's flushed face. "I

think you'd better. Wait here a minute. I'll just tell your mom where we're going."

Mandy waited impatiently. It was crunch time, time to own up to keeping Wilfred's secret.

Dr. Adam reappeared a few moments later. "Come on. We can talk on the way."

Mandy explained everything as her dad drove through Welford; how Wilfred couldn't bear to part with Matty but knew he couldn't keep her in the house much longer. And how she and James had been helping him over the past few days. "He really wanted to find a new home for her himself, Dad. To make up for getting into such a mess with his business. He says he owes it to Rose."

Dr. Adam listened intently. "So," he said when she'd finished, "you were right about Matty all along." He gave her a look. "All this explains a few things."

"Like — a bowlful of missing apples?" Mandy said, putting her chin on her chest and sliding down into her seat.

"And having hardly seen you after school for days on end. And an Animal Ark shopping bag of straw in place of a full bale, in your grandpa's shed!"

Mandy slid down farther. "Oh, you know about that, too?"

"Uh-huh, but never mind that now," her dad said. "Tell me how Matty was the last time you saw her."

Mandy smiled. Her dad never made a big deal about little things when there was something important at stake. She explained how Matty had kept shifting her weight and pawing at the ground.

"Was she looking at her sides and worrying? Trying to bite at herself?"

Mandy shook her head. "No. She seemed fine when we left."

She wished she could tell him more, but Wilfred would be able to supply other details. As soon as Dr. Adam parked the Land Rover, Wilfred rushed out of his house to greet them.

"She's pretty bad, Adam. I don't know what to do for her."

Dr. Adam clapped Wilfred on the arm. "Lead the way," he said in his calm, straightforward way.

Mandy followed them into the backroom. Matty's head hung down and her ears were laid back. She could see at once that the elderly mare's belly looked quite tight and swollen. Matty turned her head when she saw Mandy and whinnied softy, her dark eyes glazed with pain.

"Oh, you poor thing." Concern strangled Mandy's

voice. She reached up and stroked Matty's cheek soothingly, feeling relieved that her dad was here.

"Has she eaten or drunk anything recently?" Dr. Adam asked Wilfred.

Wilfred shook his head. "No. Not since yesterday when I gave her some bran mash. I found her like this, this morning."

Matty snorted restlessly, lifting each of her back feet in turn.

"Right." Dr. Adam stripped off his jacket and went into action. "Mandy, would you help me, please?"

Mandy forced herself to be practical. It helped distract her. As she opened her dad's bag and passed him his stethoscope, she found herself growing calmer. She watched Dr. Adam examine Matty with gentle, skillful hands and then listen to her stomach.

"Hmmm." Her dad stroked his dark beard thoughtfully. "I'm going to give her a painkiller," he told Wilfred. "That'll make her more comfortable. And I'm going to need blood and fluid samples from her stomach."

"Is it serious?" Wilfred asked. He put a steadying hand on Matty's neck as Dr. Adam took the samples. "There now, old girl."

Dr. Adam was screwing on tops and labeling plastic tubes. "It's not looking good, I'm afraid," he said gently.

"Do you know what's causing the colic, Dad?" Mandy

asked worriedly. She knew colic simply meant abdominal pain and that there were many reasons for it. The most serious kinds of colic could need an operation.

"We'll know more once I get the test results," her dad answered. "I'll have to go back to Animal Ark with these samples. Will you be all right here?"

Mandy smiled up at her dad. He hadn't even asked if she wanted to stay with Matty. He knew the answer already. "I'll be fine."

"Good girl." Dr. Adam patted her shoulder. "I'll be back as soon as I can."

The next couple of hours seemed like a lifetime. Matty did seem more comfortable after the painkiller, but she was still restless. Mandy and Wilfred took turns sitting with her.

To pass the time, they spoke about Rose and happier times at the stables. "Rose really loved to see the children enjoying their rides," Wilfred said with a smile. "I promised Rose I'd take care of Matty. I don't know what I'll do if anything happens to her."

"Don't worry. Dad'll help Matty," Mandy said. "He's a great vet."

"I know," Wilfred said. "He always was good. Everyone knew Tom Hope's boy was a brain."

It gave Mandy a warm feeling to think that her dad

had lived in Welford all his life. He had been born in Lilac Cottage and the townspeople thought of him as one of their own.

It was around noon when Dr. Adam returned. Mandy heard him stride into the house and dump a package on the kitchen table. "Egg and cheese sandwiches," he said. "Enough for an army. I didn't think you'd have given much thought to food. How's Matty?"

"No better," Wilfred said. "Mandy's with her. Come on in."

"What did the tests show, Dad?" Mandy asked impatiently.

"They weren't conclusive, I'm afraid," Dr. Adam replied, running an expert hand over Matty's rounded belly. "We can rule out worms. I think we're looking at impaction or a twisted gut."

Wilfred blanched. "A twisted gut. That can be fatal, can't it?"

"Oh!" Mandy gasped. Matty couldn't be about to die!

"Hold on, Wilfred," Dr. Adam said calmly. "I'm inclined to treat her for impaction."

"Does that mean something is stuck in Matty's intestines?" Mandy asked worriedly.

Her dad nodded. "That's right. Material collects there and causes a blockage. We can try to clear it out."

"But what if it *is* a twisted gut?" Wilfred said; his face

seemed carved out of stone. "Will my old girl have to have an operation?"

"Let's hope it won't come to that," Dr. Adam said, taking a length of tubing out of his bag. "Have you got a clean bucket I can use?"

"Is an operation dangerous, Dad?" Mandy whispered as she helped him mix some medication. She knew Dr. Adam believed in always telling her the truth, even though it was hard to take sometimes.

"It would be very risky at Matty's age," her dad said quietly, then in a normal voice, "Can you steady Matty while I put in the tube, Wilfred?"

Matty didn't protest as Dr. Adam put the tube in place, then fed her the medicine. Mandy patted her. "Good girl."

Dr. Adam gently withdrew the stomach tube. "Okay. The next few hours are going to be crucial. She'll need watching at all times. If she doesn't shift the blockage soon, I may have to arrange for an emergency operation."

"Can I stay here with you, Dad?" Mandy said. "If Wilfred doesn't mind."

Wilfred rubbed his unshaven cheeks. "I don't know. It could be a long job, and messy, too."

"I don't mind. I clean up messes at Animal Ark every day. Animals can't help it when they're sick." She looked up at Wilfred, her blue eyes wide and pleading. "And it would help Matty. You said yourself that she responds best to women."

Dr. Adam grinned. "Persuasive, isn't she? She could be right about Matty, though."

Wilfred nodded. "I'd be glad of any extra help. And your daughter does have a way with Matty."

Dr. Adam winked at Mandy and ushered Wilfred into the kitchen. "Put up some coffee, Wilfred," he said bracingly. "We could have a wait on our hands."

Mandy smiled to herself. Her dad had seen how tired the old man looked. It was his tactful way of getting Wilfred to relax and eat something.

"I'm going to have a chat with Wilfred in the kitchen," Dr. Adam said. "Will you monitor Matty's pulse for me?"

Mandy nodded. "And I'll call you if she starts rolling or sweating."

Mandy heard Wilfred say, "She knows her stuff."

Dr. Adam flashed Mandy one of his lopsided grins. "She's had a good teacher!"

Half an hour passed and the low rumble of voices from the kitchen continued. Mandy knew that people found it easy to talk to her dad. After all his recent troubles, Wilfred probably needed to pour his heart out.

Mandy stroked Matty, speaking soothingly to her. "Come on, girl. Get rid of all that nasty stuff that's blocking you up."

The procedure had to work soon. It just had to, otherwise her dad would have to operate. She had a horrible feeling that Matty wouldn't survive that.

Mandy rested the tips of her fingers on the artery that passed over the edge of Matty's lower jaw and counted the pulse beats. Fifty-five beats per minute. The pulse was fast, but not dangerously so.

Mandy kept checking the pulse at regular intervals. Now and then, the little mare shifted uncomfortably, her head nodding up and down. There was nothing to do but wait. Mandy tried not to give in to feelings of helplessness and fear. She spoke gently and encouragingly to Matty.

"Come on. You can do it," she repeated over and over, as if willpower alone would help shift the blockage.

After a while her eyelids started to droop. It was warm in Wilfred's living room and she hadn't slept well the previous night. Then Matty snorted and moved position. Mandy jumped, wide-awake immediately. She rested her fingers on Matty's lower jaw, feeling for the mare's pulse. Eighty beats a minute.

"Oh, no!" She ran out of the room in an instant and burst into the kitchen. "Dad! Come quickly. Matty's worse!"

Wilfred and Dr. Adam tore into the backroom, Mandy at their side. Matty had sunk to her knees. As Mandy watched, she rolled onto her side. Her breathing was shallow and her eyes rolled back in fear, as ripples threaded across her swollen belly.

Mandy threw herself down beside the mare. She cradled Matty's head in her lap as Dr. Adam examined her.

She bit her lip. "What's wrong with her, Dad?"

Dr. Adam shook his head. "It looks like the pain's getting worse and she seems to be panicking."

"No," Mandy murmured. She couldn't give up. Not now.

Her dad got up and reached for his bag. "I'm going to give her a stronger painkiller and a sedative to calm her down."

"Oh, Matty," Mandy whispered. "You *must* get well. Wilfred needs you."

Matty shuddered and raised her head, the whites of her eyes showing in pain and panic. Dr. Adam quickly gave the injection. "It'll take a moment or two to take effect."

Mandy felt tears prick her eyes as she willed the little horse not to give up. "Try. Please, try."

"Give me a hand!" Dr. Adam said to Wilfred. "Let's try to get her up. Keep on encouraging her, Mandy."

"Try to get up," Mandy urged. "Come on, Matty. Try for Rose."

Matty whinnied and heaved herself onto her knees.

"She's doing it!" Mandy said. "Good girl. Almost there!"

Matty swayed. Mandy encouraged. Dr. Adam and Wilfred pushed and pulled and finally, shakily, Matty stood up.

"Well done!" exclaimed Mandy, flinging her arms around Matty's neck.

"We're not out of the woods yet," Dr. Adam said. "I think I'd better prepare to operate —"

"No, wait!" Mandy cried. "I think it's working."

And it was. A few minutes later, the elderly mare pricked up her ears and swung around to look at Mandy. She seemed to be saying, "I did it!"

"Good girl!" Mandy said. "Look. The swelling in her stomach has all gone down."

Wilfred's wrinkled face was split in a grin. "I didn't think she'd make it. Thank goodness!"

Dr. Adam took one look around Matty's makeshift stall. He put a hand on Mandy's shoulder. "Thank goodness for your grandpa's straw!"

They all laughed with relief. No one minded the mess. The only thing that mattered was Matty: Matty looking bright-eyed and almost back to her old self.

"Better start cleaning up," Mandy said, feeling as if she could walk on air. "It'll be just like doing the chores at Animal Ark times ten!"

Dr. Adam checked Matty over thoroughly. The little mare seemed remarkably calm after her ordeal. She stood in clean straw. She had drunk some water and was now nibbling at her hay net.

"Look at her," Wilfred said fondly. He turned to Mandy. "Thanks."

"I didn't do very much," she replied, blushing.

"No need to be modest," Wilfred said stoutly. "You

gave Matty the will to keep going, just like Rose would have done."

Mandy was glad she had been able to make a difference. It was a good feeling to think that Rose would have been pleased.

Dr. Adam promised to stop by the following day, just to make sure Matty hadn't developed any other problems. "Not that I expect her to," he said to Wilfred. He waved to the old man as he and Mandy made their way to the Land Rover. "I'll think about what we said. If I hear of anything, I'll let you know."

"Sure!" Wilfred called out.

"What did you mean?" Mandy asked. "Are you going to help Wilfred find stabling for Matty?"

Her dad shook his head. "Back there, in Wilfred's kitchen, he told me how bad he felt about Matty getting sick."

"But it wasn't Wilfred's fault! Horses can get colic for all sorts of reasons."

"I know that, sweetheart. And Wilfred probably knows it, too, but I think he blames himself for being too sentimental, giving in to the impulse to keep Matty for a little while longer."

Mandy couldn't help herself. She sprang to Wilfred's defense. "But he loves Matty so much — he just couldn't bear to part with her. And Matty loves Wilfred, too, Dad!"

"I know," her dad agreed. "But now Wilfred thinks he made a bad decision. He knows it's not fair to keep Matty in the house. He has to find her a good home elsewhere. It's the only answer."

Mandy's spirits sank. "Wilfred's going to give Matty up, isn't he? And he's asked you to help him find someone to take her!"

Dr. Adam nodded. "It's probably best for everyone."

Mandy couldn't make herself believe that. What had Wilfred said? "The two of us get along okay together."

She stared out of the window. After everything that had just happened, poor Wilfred was going to lose his Matty. She felt a tightness in her throat. It wasn't fair. Life wasn't fair. There just had to be some way for Wilfred to keep Matty.

Ten

The following day was a scorchingly hot Sunday. Flora Pearson poured some water into the bright yellow mug. "There you go, Sparky."

Mandy and James grinned as the little dog lapped up the drink. They had stopped off at the pet shop in Walton earlier in the week and bought Sparky a present: a bone-shaped dog chew.

"Oh, how nice," Flora said when she saw it. "Say 'thank you' nicely now, Sparky."

Sparky scooted up onto one haunch. He sat up crookedly and gave one of his startling doggy grins. "Woof! Woof!"

"Good job," Flora exclaimed. "A perfect gentleman!"

They all laughed. "That special plastic cast works well," Flora said. "It supports his leg, but hardly restricts his movements at all."

"That's why Dad used the vetcast instead of plaster," Mandy said. "He says it's a brilliant invention."

Flora took a sip of her drink. Today she was resplendent in a blue baseball cap and a black T-shirt, which sported an enormous pink pig wearing sunglasses. The logo beneath it read, SAVE MY BACON.

Mandy and James, both wearing shorts, sprawled on the grass, drinking glasses of cool lemonade. Their bikes were propped against a tree. Sunlight shimmered on the tents and camper vans. The heat haze trembled at the edge of the field.

Flora had rolled up the bottom of her tent and flysheet, securing the fabric with plastic clothes pegs, so that cool air blew into the stuffy tent. "Sparky can't abide being hot when he's resting on his bed," she explained.

Just then, a ball came bouncing toward Flora's tent. Two young children had been kicking it to each other a few yards away. James stood up and kicked the ball back to them. "Here you are!"

"Thanks!" they called, running to pick it up, their shiny, pink faces wreathed in smiles.

"Hey!" a voice rang out. "You shouldn't be kicking that around in here. You could damage the tents!" A big man wearing green shorts and a matching shirt stood in front of a posh tent, waving angrily.

The children's faces fell. They scooped up their ball and slunk away down the field.

"That's not fair!" Mandy said. "They weren't doing any harm."

"No," Flora agreed. "There's room for them to play in this field."

Mandy looked at the children, now sitting on the grass looking bored. She thought how nice it would be if there were some activity provided for them, like a game of volleyball or swimming or maybe riding lessons.

"I wonder where Sam Western is," said James, breaking through Mandy's thoughts. He was looking toward the Range Rover that was parked down the field, near the newly converted shower block. It had been there for some time, but there had been no sign of its driver.

"If you mean the loudmouth with the jacket and his ferret-faced sidekick," Flora said with a sniff, "they're fixing one of the showers. I saw them go in a while ago."

Mandy and James grinned at each other. Flora's descriptions were colorful, but accurate. Except, Mandy thought, that she was being a bit unfair to ferrets. She was looking idly at the Range Rover when she spotted some movement in the back.

She stiffened and looked at the car more carefully. Yes, all the windows appeared to be shut. And there was the movement again.

"Did Mr. Western have his dogs with him?" she asked.

"Yes." Flora blinked at her. "Two brutish-looking bull-dogs wearing studded collars. They growled at Sparky as the car passed by him."

Mandy got to her feet. "Come on!" she yelled.

"What's wrong?" James gaped, scrambling to his feet.

"The windows are closed," she called back to him. "With the sun on it, that Range Rover will be like an oven inside."

"Oh, no!" Flora clapped her hands to her face, catching on quickly. "Those dogs!"

"We need to do something!" James sprinted after Mandy.

Mandy reached the Range Rover first. One look and her worst suspicions were confirmed. Both dogs were collapsed onto their sides, panting and wheezing. Their chests were shuddering painfully, and their tongues trailed limply from the sides of their mouths.

"It's heat exhaustion," Mandy said. "I'll get the car keys!" She ran into the old stable block.

Sam Western was talking to two campers, Dennis Saville by his side. "Quick," she yelled. "Mr. Western. Come and open your Range Rover!"

"Now just hold on a minute," began Dennis Saville, taking a step toward her.

"Please," Mandy gasped, ignoring him and grabbing Sam Western's jacket sleeve. "Your dogs have heat-stroke. They could die!"

Sam Western's ruddy face blanched. "Oh, no!" He rummaged in his pocket and produced the keys, then hurried toward the door.

"Call Animal Ark on your mobile phone," Mandy said to Dennis Saville. As soon as she saw him dialing the number, she spun on her heel and grabbed a small, plastic garbage can. Dumping the contents on the floor, she filled it with water, then charged back outside.

Moments later, Dennis Saville pounded after her. Flora and James were still standing by the Range Rover. Fingers trembling, Sam Western fitted the keys in the lock and pulled open the car door.

A wave of heat hit Mandy in the face.

"The poor things!" James murmured.

The bulldogs didn't look fierce and aggressive now, just distressed. They lay slumped in the car, their breathing labored and rasping. Their huge jaws hung open to expose swollen tongues. Mandy felt for them. She might not like their owner, but right now these dogs were just like any other patients needing help.

Suddenly, Dennis Saville shouldered her to one side. "I'll deal with this," he said curtly. "Someone give me a hand to lift them out and lay them on the grass."

"No, wait!" Mandy cried. "Please!" She jostled for position as Dennis leaned forward. "Mr. Western! First we have to lower their temperature. Right now. Or they could die!"

Saville faltered. He looked across at Sam Western. "Boss?"

Sam Western shook his head. His neat gray-blond hair stood on end. For once in his life he seemed lost for words.

"Bulldogs have breathing problems anyway," Mandy spoke fast, her eyes pleading. "This is worse for them than other dogs!"

Suddenly, a thin figure thrust itself between them. "Look here!" Flora said, taking charge. "I'd advise you two to stop blustering and let Mandy get on with helping those poor dogs! She knows what she's doing. She helped save my Sparky the other night." Without waiting for their reply, she turned to Mandy. "What can we do to help?"

Sam Western and Dennis Saville stood aside, their expressions grim.

Mandy sighed in relief. "We need cloths," she said. "Anything we can soak."

"Here you go!" Flora whipped off her huge T-shirt. She thrust it at Mandy, her skinny arms hanging out of an army surplus undershirt. James did the same.

Mandy grabbed both T-shirts, dunked them in the water she'd brought out, and laid one across each dog. "Can you open all the car doors, Mr. Western?" she said. "So that a cool breeze blows through."

"Right." Sam Western hurried around to the other car doors.

Mandy spoke softly to the stricken dogs. "Don't worry. Help's coming." One of them looked at her helplessly, a whimper rising in its throat. Mandy patted its big square head.

Someone gave her a clean handkerchief. Mandy dunked it, then dribbled a little water into the dogs' mouths, not too much or they might choke. Then she dripped water onto the wet T-shirts, keeping them cool.

"I think they're breathing easier," she said after a few minutes, wiping their faces with the wet handkerchief. The dogs were panting, their sides heaving like bellows, but the panicked look had gone from their eyes.

Sam Western had taken off his cotton safari jacket and was flapping it around, fanning the dogs. Mandy had never seen him looking so upset. He might be a pompous bully, but he obviously cared deeply for his animals.

"Your dad's here, Mandy!" James cried.

The Animal Ark Land Rover slowed to a halt and Dr. Adam jumped out. He took note of the situation in a single glance. He nodded to Sam Western, then bent over the dogs. After listening to their hearts and lungs, he straightened up.

"Will they be all right, Dad?" Mandy asked worriedly.

Her dad smiled. "I think so. You got to them just in time."

He gave each of the bulldogs a sedative to calm them down. "If you bring them to the clinic," he said to Sam Western, "I'll give them a thorough checkup."

As he was putting away the syringes, Dr. Adam looked up at Sam Western. His normally pleasant face was stern. "You ought to have known better, Mr. Western," he said. "You were minutes away from losing those dogs. Mandy's quick thinking probably saved your dogs' lives."

Sam Western's face went very red.

"I should say that a thank-you is in order," Flora prompted, digging Mr. Western hard in the ribs with a bony elbow.

"Oooof!" he groaned.

Mandy only just managed to suppress a giggle. There was a long pause. Everyone waited. Then Sam Western mumbled, "Ahem. Thank you."

It was all she was going to get, but Mandy didn't care. The dogs were alive because of her. It was the best feeling in the world. The feeling reminded her why she wanted to be a vet like her mom and dad.

Just then she noticed that the children who had been kicking the ball earlier stood by the car. They were the ones who had rushed over and thrust the handkerchief into her hand. An earlier thought came back to her. Yes! There was something important she had to ask Sam Western.

"Mr. Western," she said, making her voice calm and reasonable. "Can I ask you something?"

Western looked suspicious. "I suppose so," he said grudgingly.

Mandy took a deep breath. "It's about your campsite. You see — children don't have anything much to do here."

"Hmmph!" Western stuck his hands in his pants pockets. "I hadn't planned to make this into a vacation resort, you know! It's only temporary, until I decide what to do with the land."

Flora gave Western a sharp look. "I think you should

hear Mandy out," she said, jabbing the air with a thin finger, "after the huge favor she's just done you!"

Western glanced at Flora nervously. "Go on, then," he said to Mandy.

"Well — what about offering riding lessons?" Mandy said.

"How would I do that?"

"I think I know someone who might be able to help you out there," Mandy said. "I've got a friend who might be able to provide you with the perfect horse."

Sam Western shook his head. "Sounds like it could be a lot of trouble."

"It wouldn't be," Mandy said, warming to her theme. "I noticed that there are still two empty stalls in what was the stable block. You could let my friend use one of them for his horse. I'm sure I could persuade him to give free riding lessons to the campers. All you would have to do is provide bedding and food for his horse."

"It's a good idea," Dr. Adam said, giving his daughter a knowing smile. "In fact, it's a great idea!"

"It may be," Sam Western said abruptly. "But I'm still not convinced."

"I think you need something to attract people back to the campsite," Mandy said casually, changing tack.

"What do you mean?" Sam Western asked.

"Well — it can't be good for business — owning a

haunted campsite. Free riding lessons would be something different," Mandy said encouragingly. "And word would soon get around."

"You can't argue with that!" Flora said triumphantly.

"No!" agreed James.

He can't? Mandy thought, *I bet he'll try!* She held her breath. Would Sam Western agree? He was stroking his chin, weighing up the business sense of it. Mandy couldn't bear the suspense.

"Okay. I agree."

"Yes!" James punched the air.

Mandy's own grin spread right across her face. "That's great! Fantastic! Wait until I tell Wil, um, my friend. Oh, there's one more thing."

Sam Western sighed, but his face almost cracked into a smile. Almost. "Now why am I not surprised? Go on."

"Well," Mandy began, Sam Western and everyone else listening intently.

When she had finished speaking, Western nodded slowly. "Hmm . . . not a bad idea. Not bad at all. I like it!"

Dr. Adam lifted Mandy's bike into the back of the Land Rover. "You know," he said, giving Mandy one of his lopsided smiles, "somehow I don't think Sam Western would have been as keen on your idea for riding lessons if he had known that Wilfred was the phantom horseman!"

Mandy chuckled. "That's why I'm never going to tell him!"

"Me neither!" said James, helping Mandy's dad to slide his bike in beside Mandy's.

"Poor Ernie Bell," Mandy said thoughtfully as they drove into Welford. "He'll have nothing to gossip about, now that the mystery of the ghostly horseman has been solved."

Her dad grinned. "Oh, I don't know. I think Ernie will be tickled pink to know that Wilfred's having the last laugh on Sam Western!"

Late afternoon sunshine beamed down onto the old stable block. It was the following day. Mandy and James had rushed over to the campsite after school. There was hardly a cloud in the sky.

"A perfect day for moving in!" Mandy exclaimed.

Wilfred smiled. "It is. And it's thanks to you that we are."

Mandy patted Matty. The little mare was fully recovered; her silver-gray coat gleamed with health. She was reaching down to nibble at the grass, making soft tearing sounds.

"You should thank Sam Western," she said. "He saw that the idea made good business sense."

"Nah." Wilfred winked. "I was right the first time."

Mandy remembered his face when she first told him the news yesterday. He had looked at her in disbelief, not sure whether to laugh or cry. "Oh! That's great," was all he could say for a long time. "I can keep my Matty? Oh! That's great."

Mandy had felt a lump rise in her throat. She was happy for Wilfred and happy that she and James could visit Matty whenever they wanted.

"Should we show Matty her new home?" asked James now.

After a final check that neither Sam Western nor his men were still around, Wilfred led Matty inside the old stable block. The mare's nostrils quivered and she lifted her head, whinnying with pleasure.

"She recognizes her old home!" Mandy chuckled. "Oh, look. Isn't it great?"

And it was. A partition had been put in, so that Matty's stall was separate from the toilets and washroom area. There was sweet straw bedding, a full hay net, and fresh water. Sam Western hadn't wasted any time. His workmen must have been busy all day.

"And look!" James said. "The other empty stall's become a grooming room!"

"Oh." Mandy looked with delight at the straps hanging on hooks, the rack holding saddle soap, cloths, and brushes. Matty's saddle was slung across a sort of bench, topped by a sloping bar. It was perfect. Absolutely perfect.

"Western's outdone himself," Wilfred said gruffly. "I'd never have believed it."

"It's because of his dogs," said James. "It's his way of saying thanks."

Perhaps it was. Mandy felt embarrassed. She changed the subject. "There's something else, Wilfred. You were too busy with Matty to notice it as we came through the campsite gate. But come and see. Both of you."

Wilfred followed Mandy, Matty at his side. He looked spry and dapper, in corduroy pants and a dark green vest. His white hair was combed back and a mustard scarf was tucked into the neck of his shirt.

Mandy led Wilfred and Matty back to the campsite entrance. James followed, grinning. Together they pointed to the newly-painted sign next to the gate.

"Ta-da!" they shouted.

The sign read, ROSE OF YORKSHIRE CAMPSITE."

Wilfred's face glowed. He swallowed hard. "Oh! I can't believe it!"

"Sam Western thought my idea to change the campsite's name made sense," Mandy explained. "It would stop people from thinking about it being haunted."

"A new name, a new beginning, huh?" Wilfred said with a wink. "Western can think what he likes, but we know who this campsite's named after. Don't we, Matty? *Our* Rose!"

The little mare nodded, her ears swiveling. She whinnied and blew gently, then butted her nose against Wilfred's vest.

"Looks like Matty's given her new home her seal of approval!" Mandy said and she laughed out loud.

ANIMAL ARK

Where animals come first

Look for Animal Ark®:
PONY IN A PACKAGE

After filling up Gabriel's evening water bucket and shaking out some more straw onto his bed in the shed, Mandy sat in a chair on the patio and watched him grazing his way slowly around the yard. She dug her hands deep into her pockets. It was cold but she wanted to make the most of every minute of having Gabriel there.

The little horse's teeth made a rhythmical tearing, chewing sound as he ripped up the grass. His ears twitched and his tiny hooves stamped into the lawn.

Whose horse are you? Mandy thought as she watched him work his way nearer and nearer to where she was sitting. "Good boy," she murmured as the little horse reached the edge of the patio. Daintily, he stepped onto the patio and walked right up to her. She reached out to stroke him and he nuzzled at her hair. She giggled and ducked. "It's my hair, Gabriel! Not hay!"

"An easy mistake," Dr. Emily said, coming out of the house and onto the patio. She ruffled Mandy's untidy hair and patted Gabriel's neck. "He's adorable, isn't he?"

Mandy grinned. "And so friendly."

"Miniature horses normally are," said Dr. Emily. "They love people and they make great companions."

Gabriel wandered back onto the grass and for a while they both watched him. Then Mandy sighed and turned to her mother. "Where do you think he came from, Mom? And who do you think he belongs to?"

Dr. Emily put her hand gently around Mandy's shoulders. "I guess we'll find out tomorrow."

Mandy nodded and looked at Gabriel. Yes, Mom was right. Tomorrow they would find out.

The post office was still not open when Mandy left for school the next morning. "I'll call them later," Dr. Emily promised her. "And then we should be able to sort out this mix-up."

Mandy went around to the yard. "Bye, Gabe," she

whispered, kissing his soft nose. He tickled her cheek with his lips and she felt her heart twist at the thought that he might not be there when she got home.

Dr. Emily opened the patio door. "Mandy! You'll be late."

With one last look at Gabriel, Mandy got on her bike and rode through the town to the Fox and Goose crossroads to meet James. He wasn't there. She stopped her bike by the curb and waited. Her mind was full of thoughts of Gabriel. Who was this Tania Benssomething who owned him and where did she live?

"Mandy!" A voice broke into her thoughts. A boy came hurrying toward her out of the Fox and Goose restaurant.

"John!" she said in surprise. "Hi! I didn't know you were home."

"Our last day was on Friday," John Hardy said. "Dad picked me up on Saturday. That's the good thing about boarding school. We have longer vacations!"

John went to a boarding school in the Lake District. Mandy had first become friendly with him a couple of vacations ago. "How are Button and Barney?" she asked. "Do you have them at the moment, or has Imogen?"

"I do. Dad and I got them yesterday." Button and Barney were two rabbits that John shared with Imogen

Parker-Smythe. John looked after them during vacations whenever Imogen was away, and Imogen looked after them when John was at school. Mandy thought it was a very good deal because it meant that the two rabbits got lots of love and attention all the time.

"You'll have to come and see them," John told her, pushing a hand through his dark hair. "I'm keeping them *all* vacation." His eyes shone with pleasure. "Imogen's got a new pony and she's going to be busy with that for the next few weeks."

"Oh, yes!" In the excitement of having Gabriel around Mandy had virtually forgotten about Star, Imogen's new pony. "Have you seen the pony?"

"Just briefly," said John. He shrugged dismissively. "It was sort of gold-colored." He returned to a subject that interested him more. "You should see how much Button and Barney have grown. I'm going to make each of them a little stocking with rabbit treats for Christmas. You *must* come and see them."

"I will," promised Mandy. She saw James biking at great speed toward them and got back on her bike. "I'd better go or we'll be late for school. *Some* of us haven't gotten out yet. I'll call you when we do. Only another five days to go!"

James screeched up behind her as she started off.

"Sorry, Mandy!" he gasped, pushing his glasses back up his nose. "I overslept!"

"What's new?" Mandy grinned. "Come on, I'll race you up the hill."

Once at school, Mandy and James went to their separate classes. "See you later!" Mandy called, slinging her bag onto her shoulder. Ms. Potter, her teacher, hated anyone being late.

But today it was Ms. Potter who was late. "You're lucky!" Susan Collins said, looking at the clock as Mandy thankfully sat down at the desk next to her. "How's Gabriel?" But before Mandy could answer, Ms. Potter came into the classroom. With her was a girl with blonde hair whom Mandy didn't recognize. The girl glanced quickly around the class and then dropped her eyes to the floor.

There was a hasty shuffling of chairs and the sound of desks lids closing. "Good morning, class!" said Ms. Potter, putting her bag down on the desk and adjusting her large, round glasses.

"Good morning, Ms. Potter," the class replied. Mandy looked curiously at the girl. Who was she? Her shoulder-length hair fell like a curtain across Her face.

Ms. Potter smiled at the class. "Well, everyone, I

would like you to meet your new classmate, Tania Benster."

Mandy almost jumped out of her seat in surprise. *Tania Benster!* Just like the name on Gabriel's crate!

"Tania will be starting school with us after Christmas," continued Ms. Potter, "and so she is going to spend this week getting to know you all and getting to know the school." She pointed to an empty desk behind Mandy. "Go ahead and take that spare seat there, Tania."

Tania walked down the row of desks. The people she passed looked curiously at her but she stared at the floor, not meeting their eyes. Reaching the empty place she sat down.

Mandy swung eagerly around in her seat. "Do you . . . ?"

"No talking, please, Mandy," Ms. Potter interrupted, her voice firm. "Turn around. I want to take the attendance. You'll have plenty of time to get to know Tania later."

Mandy had to sit through attendance, almost bursting with excitement. She was longing to ask Tania about Gabriel. Was she his owner? Unable to resist a quick glance over her shoulder, Mandy saw that the new girl had taken a notebook out and was drawing on the cover. Mandy twisted around further to see what she was drawing. It was a horse! At that moment, Tania looked up. Seeing Mandy watching her she quickly covered her drawing with her arm.

Mandy was about to whisper something when Susan nudged her. Ms. Potter had just read out Mandy's name for the second time. "Here, Ms. Potter!" Mandy said, swinging around hastily to face the front.